A New Season

The End to Man's Reign

A New Season

The End to Man's Reign

S.A. Patterson

A New Season
The End to Man's Reign

© S.A. Patterson 2018

This book is a work of fiction. Named locations are used fictitiously, and characters and incidents are the product of the author's imagination. Any resemblance to actual events or places or persons, living or dead, is entirely coincidental.

Published by
Lighthouse Christian Publishing
SAN 257-4330
5531 Dufferin Drive
Savage, Minnesota, 55378
United States of America

www.lighthousechristianpublishing.com

Prologue

Since the beginning of time, there has been a continuous struggle for the dominion of the earth and its peoples. Perceived by man as a struggle of good versus evil, as man himself has always been the prize to be won. One side offers the promise of man's freedom, and the other promises fairness under the rule of a dominating governing body. Each age of man has faced these challenges, as the seeds of dominance have repeatedly sprung up to challenge the hope of freedom.

****

Around the turn of the twentieth century, a new seed of darkness was cast upon the world of man, birthed in the citadels and ivory towers of pride and arrogance, by people who called their institutions places of "higher learning." The seed grew in the hearts of arrogance among the ranks of the world's elites, rapidly spreading across societies. But to prevent fear from among those "less enlightened" people, the elites gave the seed an unassuming name: "Socialism."

The spiritual forces that spawned the seed granted it four shoots (or offspring) with each shoot becoming a political ideology. Each ideological shoot held a greater darkness than its preceding siblings. Like strangle vines, these ideologies grew within the hearts of their successive peoples, robbing them of heart and individual freedoms.

In Italy, the shoot was named "Fascism" and was much admired around the world at that time. Their leader stood as a king, although his title was much less imposing, so as not to frighten the common people. But as the weak always submit to the greater force, the darkness of Fascism submitted to the greater darkness of Germany's "Naziism." The Nazi party rose up in the fledgling democracy of Germany, calling itself "the party of the people." The great political and social machine of the party showed the world just how far a socialistic government could go. The Nazi party imposed a power over its people that would put some of the most tyrannical kings to shame. At its end, Naziism fell to the insanity spawned of man, submitting to an even greater darkness than itself. Thus, the budding empire fell into ruin, death, and destruction.

The third shoot from this branching, vine-like growth, snaked its way to the lands of the East. This branch, being slightly more subtle than its brother in Germany, moved slower, yet truer, in its domination over its people. And its darkness was called "Communism." A force that would grow up to establish two mighty empires. Both of which were more cruel in their darkness than any free man could have comprehended prior to their rise. For these empires turned in upon themselves, consolidating their power, always probing for weaknesses among the surrounding peoples of the world.

Finally, the fourth shoot gave rise to its own spawn. An ocean away from its three siblings, this spawn truly did expand in its growth like the most cunning serpent. The adherents called their movement "Progressivism." After all, what could be wrong with progressing society? Although this seed saw its brothers with jealousy, this seed grew among a different kind of people. Unlike those in Europe, the people of America had been raised up believing in the natural order that allowed man to live free. Thus, this darkness had to work slowly and subtly to strangle the liberty from the hearts and minds of the American people. Another difference from their European counterparts: the American people had a constitution and laws under which they lived, and they believed in the rule of law and the liberty it assured. The laws of America were based upon the spiritual concepts found within biblical teachings. And the Bible of the Christian faith stood in direct contrast to the growing serpent of darkness.

Once the serpent rose, exposing itself to the peoples of America, the people were repulsed. As the people stood up to repel the beast, defending their rights and liberties, the beast fell and became as dead in the eyes of the people. But like the mythical Hydra, when the head of the beast had been severed, the body simply slithered off into the darkness of political obscurity. There, the beast lay waiting, growing many heads in place of the first.

Over the ensuing decades, the many heads of this insidious beast snaked their way into the many aspects of American society, especially targeting those aspects which had previously led to its initial downfall.

The movement saw the churches as being especially dangerous. For the very Word that they taught was a direct affront to the beast and its darkness. So the church was one of the beast's major targets, infecting seminaries, stimulating denominational divides, and providing government monies through the tax code. Like the serpent, the beast hissed into the ears of church leaders with lies to separate them from the political aspects of their society. They were told that if the government couldn't interfere with the church, then the church couldn't interfere with the government. Once this step-child of the beast was planted, it prospered in the fertile soil of men's minds, growing within the many churches to become a self-propagating creature of its own. The living lie grew to imply that the church, and therefore religion, must be vanquished from all aspects of society.

To answer that deeply inbred need for spiritual purpose, this growing step-child of the beast provided a new kind of spirituality. Many called this new movement "Humanism." Although it was never more than a step-child of the beast that lurked behind the scenes. And while the church was deluding itself into oblivion, the enemies of Christ and His church were establishing an army within the political structure, to enforce an imposition against the Christian religion. One of the many branches of this politically sponsored army was even given the unassuming name of the "American Civil Liberties Union." After all, what could be wrong with civil liberty?

The second head of the beast snaked its way into the educational systems of America. During its initial exposure to the people of America, the beast had ignored the general populace. Now, it realized that the spirit of the "little" people had too strong a spirit to be ignored. Books and histories were rewritten with the eye of the serpent, and thus, the great deception began. No longer were the founding fathers of America seen as the visionaries they were. They were marked as short-sighted little men who were accused of the very sins the progressives sought to resurrect. Many trials and battles (both in the halls of government as well as the battlefields) were fought in the earlier years of America. Battles to abolish slavery, and to assure that the American constitution applied to all men as it was intended. But the lies of the beast endured, convincing the poor and under-educated that the founders sought to keep slavery as a revered institution. At the same time, the servants of the beast were working to institute a new kind of slavery, creating racial division and strife among the classes of peoples in America. All to bring the nation to the point of chaos and thus, conquest.

The political head had changed its colors and shape, although its heart and venom remained the same. Moving through the shadows of our political system, the progressives infiltrated first the one party that held those values closest to its own. Then, election by crafted election, the progressives began to infiltrate the opposing political party, assuring a continued movement along the desired path toward total domination of the American people.

In the 1960's, the beast thought that it had made the necessary gains to rise again. The result was an America experiencing a decade of chaos at the hands of the servants of the beast. With radicals preaching the lie that America was an empire that must be resisted, instead of the Republic that it was in reality. A revolution was started to replace the government of and for the people with a utopian, socialistic dream. Although the beast failed in the attempted revolution of the 60's and 70's, it learned much. And its servants moved into new positions to effect an even greater revolution at a "more opportune time." More importantly, the beast had not tipped its hand, exposing its rising power within the political system.

To carry on the fight, a new head began to snake its way even deeper into society. Although, in truth, this serpent had been there since the beginning, its role had always been minor. Now, the beast began moving through the economic and industrial sectors in the name of organizing for the welfare of the people. The lie it stood upon was that people needed to have organized groups to protect them and to subjugate the "evil rich," lest the people be exploited. Organizations were established to unify the working man. But as the workers turned their attentions back to the task of living their lives, the leaders were gradually replaced with those more in tune with the will of the beast. Thus, silencing the individual, taking his voice out of the political and economical realms.

By the turn of the twenty-first century, the beast had come full circle, growing upon itself, and using its own unwitting slaves to rise up against the cause of freedom and liberty. It had the unstated goal of subjugating the American people to the progressive cause, and creating a yoke of bondage for anyone capable of living in this new society. For those deemed too rooted in their ways, or too un-enlightened to accept the new world order, there are always camps to reeducate or, if necessary, exterminate these less enlightened people.

CHAPTER 1

The Great Calling

A faint breeze blew through the front room window as Stan Robinson relaxed on the couch, watching the Sunday morning edition of the local news-cast. He could hear the sounds of his wife getting ready for church in the next room. But Stan's attention was completely on the news-cast this morning. The lead-in to the broadcast had been: "PRESIDENTIAL HOPEFUL FOUND DEAD...THIS AND OTHER STORIES TO FOLLOW," without name or circumstances involved being mentioned. This had Stan's full attention. With so few in the governmental race that he could truly respect, he had to know which one it was. After what seemed to be an unusually long stretch of commercials, the news-cast finally began with their cover story. Stan felt his heart sink, as they announced that Presidential hopeful William

Jefferson was found dead, along with his family, in their Atlanta home. A portrait of William Jefferson, with his stern and determined expression, filled the screen behind the news-anchor man Thomas Alderman, as he read the script to the audience: "The cause of death is believed to be that of an unknown disease, being called by some 'the plague.' Authorities have released the evidence that the contortions of the bodies were, indeed, characteristic of this unidentified disease." Stan's mind drifted for a time, as the news-cast continued.

"It doesn't look like God's going to pull us out of the frying pan this time," Stan whispered to himself, as he heard his wife calling from the other room, asking what was going on.

All the while, the news-cast continued with its ever-irrelevant storylines. Paying closer attention that he might be able to explain to his wife, Stan heard Thomas Alderman announce, "From his tower of meditation, to announce his latest revelation, we take you now to the campus for 'The Church of Modern Christian Theology,' where our reporter Harry Swenson, has that story."

From the screen behind the anchor, could be seen the reporter, standing before one of the campuses' many impressive buildings. As if on cue, the small screen expanded to fill the television's screen, just as the reporter began to speak: "Thank you, Thomas. Not thirty minutes ago, the religious community got another chastising by the Reverend Norm Richardson, in one of his more spectacular presentations, from the tower of meditation itself." With a back-drop of the very public preacher speaking to a massive crowd, the reporter continued: "Reverend Richardson has declared that his seclusion has revealed the reasons for *the plague* the world is facing. He claims that the plague is 'Gods wrath on those who follow the deceptively false prophets of modern psychology.'" A skeptical smile found its way to the reporter's face as he continued: "And on those who have neglected in their supporting of the true church, he cites the inability of the medical community to come up with an explanation as to what the actual disease is, and the apparent randomness of its strikes, as proof." The red face of the preacher bespoke of his intensity, as he shouted out at one of the largest crowds ever shown to assemble at the campus.

As the preacher's voice began to be heard by the viewers, the camera brought the man's face into a close-up view: "We must above all else, support the church! It is in this neglect that God is so displeased with us all! It is our self-centered greed that first brought the failure of the church in our country! And now, the country is feeling the financial distress that it has placed on the church. But have we listened? NO! Have we tried to make right what we have done to our churches? NO! So now, God has given us something that we can't ignore-*The Plague*!" As Norm Richardson continued his shouted sermon to the crowd, Stan felt a chill run down his spine. Not for what was being said, but rather by the picture of the preacher's face. For although his facial expressions and motions seemed to express the intensity of his emotional outpouring, the man's eyes seemed to have a stone-cold life of their own. For a man who spent his week working in the psychiatric ward of a local hospital, Stan felt that he was looking into the face of insanity itself.

The preacher's face and voice had faded, as the picture pulled back to show the full crowd, then switched back to the reporter. Harry Swenson gave his closing comment before returning the broadcast back to the news-desk: "And I guess for a reasonable amount, he's offering protection from his God's plague." Thomas Alderman had the same mocking smile that his reporter had. A smile that vanished as quickly as it had come, as he turned away from that story's monitor, back to the audience, and the more serious stories to follow.

As the news-man began the lead-in to the story of a massive earthquake that had struck southern California in the night, Stan's wife, Sally, came into the room, brushing her long, brown hair into perfection atop the most beautiful face Stan had ever known. He leaned back on the couch to watch her as she came in. Even after six years together, his enjoyment in watching his wife preparing for the day hadn't lessened one bit. Even the frown that was on her face as she looked at the television, didn't lessen his feelings at the moment. He was only partially listening, as she was saying in a disgusted voice, "I can't believe the way people are anymore. A few years ago, if someone had used such crass language toward the Lord, they would be off the air before the broadcast ended. The way things are now, I doubt anybody even heard what he said." Shaking her head, she turned back to Stan, adding, "But then, I doubt we had preachers whose actions would encourage that kind of thing. Speaking of actions, don't you think you should get ready? I really would hate to be late for church this morning."

Stan seemed to come to life, as his wife bent over to give him a quick kiss. Hurrying into the next room to finish getting dressed for church, he forgot the coffee he had been drinking in the other room. His thoughts, as he slipped on a sports jacket and returned to where his wife was waiting, kept going back to the day they met. Taking her hand as they walked out to the car, he said, "Every day is like the first time we met."

Smiling as she got in the car, she waited for him to get in before she asked him, "I feel the same, but what brought it up?" She looked over at Stan with a questioning expression on her face, as he started the car up and began the short drive to church in silence.

"I don't know," Stan began, as though the minutes of silence hadn't existed, "I just feel good all of sudden, and when I feel good, I think of you. And that always makes me feel the way I did, that day I walked into the store and saw you behind the counter." After a moment of smiling silence, he added, "Isn't the day a beautiful day?"

As they drove through the community of Tucamill, they both took time to pay attention to the world around them. It had rained the night before, and the air had a crisp freshness to it, as it moved barely enough to shift the leaves into a slow motion dance on the trees. While the large billowed clouds drifted slowly across the sky, like huge mountains making their way across a dream. Stan realized that they had slowed to a coasting speed without intending to. But no one else was on the road, so he decided to just enjoy the ride. The yards of the homes they passed seemed to have come to life overnight. It was a route he took every day of the week, but he couldn't remember it being so much alive with color. The spring flowers, that had been late in coming this year, were in full bloom, alongside the flowering shrubs that usually waited until mid-summer to come to their full potential. The air was so full of the scents from the wide variety of blooming color, he almost wished that they had time to stop and take in the morning. Even at the slow speed they traveled, they soon found themselves pulling into the church's parking lot.

Usually, Sally would be in a hurry to get into the church, rather than risk being late. But all she said on this morning was, "You're right. It is beautiful this morning". The regular crowd hung outside the church's front door, engaged in the typical small talk. Stan and Sally took a few minutes to join in, before going inside. There was the usual gossip that always seemed to go around whenever a large group of townspeople got together. But there seemed to be a kind of excitement in the air - almost as if the air itself had an expectation to it, hanging on every word spoken.

Stan had little time to puzzle over the feeling, when his friend Bill Horton, the small church's pastor, stepped out of the door and motioned the crowd to enter in. There was something about Bill that made Stan wonder if he, too, could feel the excitement in the air. Bill was always the happy sort, never one to let anything get to him or get him down. But the smile that seemed to radiate on his face this morning was brighter than anything Stan had ever seen. Following on the tail of the crowd, Stan paused at the door for a quiet exchange with his friend, while the others were finding their seats. "And what canary did this cat eat?" Stan began. "I hope you don't mind my saying, Brother Bill, but it looks like you've been up to something."

Stan immediately regretted his light-hearted approach, as Bill looked into his eyes. But he had definitely touched on something. For Bill looked at him with all seriousness, as if he had been asked one of the most serious questions of his life, and replied, "You know, there's something in the air. I can feel it. I'm not sure I can even explain it myself...but something happened this morning...that I can't help but feel is so very important. Ever since I got up this morning...I've felt closer to God than I ever thought possible. I think even closer than the day I gave my life to Him...Funny thing that, I've always found it easiest to prepare my sermons during the times that I felt the closest. But I haven't been able to so much as put a single word to paper. I thought I would just have to leave it to the Lord's directions,...and you know what? The very instant I made that decision, I had the funniest feeling, it was as though the Lord was telling me that He was going to take care of everything. And the feeling wasn't just, 'don't worry about the sermon.' I've had that before..." Bill was shaking his head. He had wanted someone to talk to about how he felt, and it was obvious to Stan that he wasn't quite sure himself. In almost a whisper, he finished, "I just can't explain, it's so new..." Then with a motion toward Sally, he added in his natural voice, one that could easily carry across the mumble of muted conversations, "You'd better find your seat. It looks like you have someone waiting."

Stan hurried to his wife's side to begin what turned out to be a surprising search. In the six years that they had attended the small country church, this was the first time that he could remember having trouble finding a seat. His mind had been filled with the puzzle of what he had heard, until he realized that they were already a third of the way from the back of the church, before Sally was asking for room to sit. He was shocked to notice that the little church had, at least, a capacity crowd. He could remember being told at one time that their church could hold as many as three hundred if it had to. But as he looked around, he realized that not only could he not see any empty seats, there were people standing in the corners as well. Good Ole Brother Bill-he seemed oblivious to it all, as he walked up the middle aisle, greeting members and visitors alike as he always did.

One of the people that caught Stan's eye was an older lady who frowned, rather than return Bill's greeting. Stan had to think a bit before he remembered who the lady was-Fern Gilten. She hadn't been in church, not since before her husband died five years ago. She had always been very short-tempered with anyone from the church, saying that they didn't have time for her husband, so she didn't have time for them. For her to be in church was more of a shock to Stan than seeing the rest of the crowd. But then, Stan's attention was drawn away from that thought, to the front of the auditorium.

Bill had reached the pulpit and gave a warm welcome to the full congregation. Stan knew Bill well enough to know that each word, however rehearsed it sounded, was truly heartfelt. And the words he spoke this morning seemed to be a little warmer than usual. But before Stan could give much thought to those the welcome was given for, his eyebrows were raised by a surprise announcement by Bill: "Before I go on with the morning announcements, I would like to apologize to the men's Sunday school class. Things seemed to get a little out of hand this morning. I realize that it wasn't quite the traditional way for a lesson to be handled. I hope that those who were offended will forgive me. But mostly, I hope we all learned something new."

'Just like Bill,' Stan thought, *'more worried about what people learn than his own job. I'd think he'd realize how stiff the thinking is around here. I wonder what it was that happened? I'll have to ask after church.'* Looking around, Stan spotted several of the men who attended that class. Some of them had sheepish grins, while some of the others looked like they had eaten something that didn't agree with them. Stan had to admit that the sour-looking men tended to be that way anyway. Like Rodney McDoule and Andrew Willards, they have always had a bone to pick with Brother Bill. Still, Stan couldn't help but think, *'What on earth could have happened in there?'* Suddenly, Stan realized that the announcements were over and the choir was in the middle of its introductory song with Brother Danny Hankins, the music director, standing where Bill had just been. He was leading the singing with his customary flourish of action. That always made Stan think that the big man must have wanted to be an orchestra conductor. Over to one side, Bill sat, not seeming to enjoy the music as usual, but rather deep in prayer. Bill's Bible sat on the seat next to him, other than in his lap as it customarily did. And his face was buried deep in his hands, as if he sat alone. Brother Danny seemed oblivious to everything but his music, until the choir had finished. With all the flare of an actor making a grand entrance, the big man spun and bowed to the

approval of the congregation. "Thank you...Thank you," he called out in all his pride. "It's amazing what an audience can do for the heart. I don't think we've ever performed for such a beautiful crowd before. So, my thanks is as much for you, as to you." There were some snickers, along with the shuffling of embarrassed church members, that filled the silence.

Stan grumbled to Sally as much to himself. He had always disliked the flash and flare that Danny liked to use. Both Stan and Sally felt that those kinds of acts didn't belong in the church. But Sally ignored it all. When Stan looked over at her, she seemed intently waiting. As if she knew something was going to happen. With this much of a hint, he looked back to the pulpit just in time to catch the action as it began. No sooner had the music director asked the congregation to turn to page 218, "He Hideth My Soul," than Brother Bill was out of his seat. He looked as confused about his own actions as those watching. It looked to Stan more like he had been thrown from his seat rather than simply jumping up. When Danny realized the people's attention was no longer on him, he slowly turned around to face Bill. Brother Bill was always a little shy when talking to people. A shyness that evaporated only when he would begin to preach. But his shyness seemed to stand out even more than usual as this preacher, whose slight frame stood only five foot six, looked up at the massive build of the music director. "Do you think..." Bill began hesitantly. "I mean...would it be alright if we sang... 'To God Be the Glory?'" From where Stan sat, it looked like his friend Bill was standing on the edge of something. Even with the customary uncertainty that he would show from time to time, he seemed to speak with an authority that he had seldom shown.

Brother Danny was never one to care for impromptu changes. This one even less than most, because it interrupted *his* music. With a "humph" and a great show of irritation, Danny turned to the appropriate page. Then he announced the change to the congregation as though he were granting a favor to an errant child. Even Danny seemed somewhat surprised by the congregation's response in the opening chords of the song. The first time, for as far back as Stan could remember, the congregation led the choir into the opening chords. Nor could the choir seem to catch up with the jubilant singing of the congregation. Stan felt himself swept along with the unadulterated joy that seemed to have the entire church in its sway. With the dying of the last chord, Stan could feel a let-down of an almost physical nature. He wasn't sure he could have explained it, if asked. Before Danny had time to recover from the surprising quality of the song, Bill was back on his feet and at Danny's elbow complimenting him on the effect his leadership had on the music: "That was beautiful, Danny. I don't think I have ever heard that song done so well." As Danny muttered, "of course," Bill was already continuing, "I realize...I know...we usually have more, but...I feel so inspired by that song that I don't feel I could contain myself any longer. Let's forgo the normal formalities, just this once."

Danny was so caught off-guard by Bill's abnormal behavior, as well as the suddenness of the request, that he managed to murmur agreement without even realizing what had happened. From where Stan sat, he could see the resentment on Danny's face as he returned to his seat. But Stan's attention was quickly drawn away from the music director back to Bill, as the pastor launched into his sermon. From the moment he opened his mouth, Stan could tell that something was different. Looking around, he could tell that others sensed the change in Bill as well. Nowhere in the presentation, could be heard the self-conscious and often timid pastor that Stan had known for the past five years. The man who stood before the congregation seemed somehow larger than life. His manner and speech was that of familiarity, confidence and authority, as he called out to each and every one there to give their heart and soul to the Lord. He spoke of the glories of heaven, much as one would talk about their own home, as if from personal experience. Stan, like so many of the members of the church, had his total attention on Bill. Bill had somehow been transformed from the humblest person he had ever known to a charismatic giant in the blink of an eye. In mid-sentence, Bill interrupted himself with a start. An engaging smile spread across his face as he held out his right hand in almost a pleading gesture saying, "Don't be afraid. There is never a wrong time to answer God's call."

Looking around, Stan saw the object of his pastor's attention. The two brothers Josh and Dean Anderson did indeed look scared, if not terrified. They appeared to look nothing like the "hooligans" the older women of the church, at least those in the know, said they were. It was said that nothing bad ever happened around town without one or both being involved. At least that was the local gossip. What Stan saw was two terrified kids holding each other's hand in a near-death grip. From his vantage point, Stan could see the whites of the boys' knuckles. Stan couldn't help but feel sadness for the boys. Especially when a gasp from one of the older members at sight of them, nearly set them running.

"Please don't be afraid. It's God Himself who is calling you, not me or anyone else here today. He has something for both of you. I can feel the sadness of the Lord wanting to give you His peace, if you'll just let Him. Come...He's waiting for you." And with a gentle wave of his arm, Brother Bill indicated a place off to one side of the front for the two boys to go.

As they slowly continued down the main aisle, Bill returned his attention to the congregation. Although he spoke out to the enlarged congregation, Stan could see his pastor's eyes returning time and again to the two boys making their way to the front, with a smile that wouldn't fade as he continued. The boys reached the side of the altar and were met by Bill's wife, Amy. Bill doubled his intensity with a point that might have been too sensitive just moments before. "Don't let the time pass you by. We are all children in His sight. Don't let fear or pride stand in your way. Josh and Dean have shown more courage than I have seen in many of my own flock. They had the courage to brave a world they know little of, to answer God's call. What about you...? Don't be like the rich man who was afraid to let go of his riches in 'Matthew.' When Christ said, *'It is easier for a camel to go through the eye of a needle than for a rich man to enter the kingdom of God,'* He wasn't just speaking of the wealthy. He was speaking to each and every one of us. We're often too afraid to let go of what we have, to answer God's call."

Glancing over, Stan saw Amy kneeling with one boy on either side, praying. Her arms covered each young man's shoulder protectively, almost in a maternal way. They seemed oblivious to Bill's message, even as the apparent sobs seemed to be settling down.

Stan's attention had been off of Bill while he watched the two boys down front, losing track of the most spectacular sermon that he had ever experienced. Glancing about, Stan hoped to catch some sign of what the people thought as to what was happening. Where he had expected to see joy, or at least pleasure, what he found was quite different. The deep displeasure on Brother Danny's face was more than obvious from the seat behind Bill. Off to one side of the sanctuary, deacons

Rodney McDoule and Andrew Willards stood with arms crossed and looks of displeasure, if not outright anger, glued to their faces. Then, a slight murmur jerked Stan's attention back to Bill, whose face seemed to glow with a radiant smile, as he continued to speak. But the words were lost to Stan, as he saw the cause for the murmuring. For Fern Gilten was slowly making her way to the front. Tears left streaks in the heavy makeup she wore, as she blinked them out of her eyes. Stan, like so many others, felt the shock of seeing her in church, much less coming forward.

"Stern Fern,"as she was often called around the community, had not set foot in a church in over fifteen years, and had even campaigned against the church since her husband had died. He had always been a likable-enough person, but he drank. Then when he died, and Fern had asked to have the funeral in the local church, the pastor at the time refused. He said that we had to take a stand against "the sin of the bottle." In response, Fern had become a solitary and bitter old woman, who said that she "had no place in her life for a bunch of hypocrites or their God!" Stan had not been in the church back then, but he had experienced her hatred on the few times that he had tried to witness to her. And he had been told by a few of the older church members how she had tried to get the church closed down, on several occasions, over the years. So, it was no wonder that there was surprise seeing her there.

As Fern neared the front, Stan saw Bill give a smiling nod to Gertrude, one of the elderly widows of the church, who got up and made her way to the front. The two women embraced, as they met at the front pew and slowly got down to their knees to pray, while Bill continued. In the short time that it took the two ladies to get down to their knees, Stan could see the tears of joy that streamed down Gertrude's face. And Stan remembered hearing that the two had been friends years ago, before the conflict of the funeral tore them apart.

For two and a half hours, Bill preached. One minute, Bill would be pleading with tear-filled eyes and a voice strained from his intensity, that each and every one there must surrender. That they needed to let the Lord have their lives. While the next minute, Bill would be beaming with joy, as he spoke of the glories that the Lord was holding out for us. All we had to do was accept them. And all the while, people were making their way forward. The thought occurred to Stan that if the choir had been dismissed to their seats, as they normally would have, there wouldn't have been enough room for those going forward. As it turned out, the first three rows, normally reserved, were filled with those coming forward and those who knelt at their side. For each one that came forward, someone seemingly at random would rise up and meet them. And wherever the two would meet, they would kneel together and begin to pray.

A few of the deacons stood off to one side in silent protest, rather than meet those coming forward as would be their normal duty. Stan, noticing them at one point, thought it must be terrifying to them to see the normal, orderly service cast aside with no regard for proper ceremony.

Still, Stan's thoughts could not stay off of what Bill was saying for long. Like a powerful magnet, the words seemed to have a life of their own, as they continued to pour from Bill's mouth - a magnet that seemed to reach out into the very heart of the congregation, pulling all who cared to hear into the moment. At one point, Stan felt that it was as if his friend wasn't even there, but rather some life-sized puppet that moved and spoke at another's command. Of course if that were so, Stan felt sure that only the Lord Himself could pull those strings.

Then suddenly, without warning, it ended. A strange ghostly silence filled the air. Bill was breathing heavily and gripping the pulpit as if for support, as he continued looking out over the congregation. Something inside told Stan that Bill's eyes were not seeing the church, but something else, something spiritual perhaps. "Brothers...Sisters..." began Bill, his voice somehow changed. He sounded tired and distant, maybe. The pleading sound in his voice was that which Stan knew so well from their few years of friendship. Bill had somehow been returned to finish the sermon on his own: "Don't wait...don't let this chance pass you by. I would like each and everyone of you to kneel or bow where you are and pray. It is true the Scriptures say, *'no one knows that day or hour, not even the angels in heaven, nor the Son, but only the Father.'* But that doesn't mean that Christ won't come during our lives...and if that day comes, and we're not ready...Where do you think we will be? **It will be too late!** So, I ask you. No, I beg you. Please, if you don't have Christ as your Lord and master today, don't wait. Don't hesitate. You may never get another chance. Pray to Christ. Ask Him into your heart today. There comes a time when we all must face the possibility of a last call. Just like for a train before it pulls out of the station, this could be your last call. Please don't wait. Don't be left behind." Bill closed his eyes while everyone knelt where they were. And when quiet once again filled the church, he added, "And for those of you who have already given your lives to our Lord,...I can never begin to tell you how my heart feels, knowing that when that day comes, we'll be together with the Lord in Paradise. I ask you to remember your brothers and sisters. Pray for those around you, pray the Spirit to touch their heart. Pray that they join us in the joy we have found with Christ." With that said, Bill slowly let himself down to the floor, using the pulpit for support, where he knelt to pray.

Stan had caught a glimpse of Danny retaining his seat, even as those left in the choir knelt. His face was frozen in an expression of displeasure. But as Stan knelt beside Sally, his mind quickly dismissed thoughts of the music director and shifted to that of prayerful silence. He knelt there in silence, waiting for Brother Bill to begin to lead in the prayer. But the silence stretched on. Finally, Stan decided that they were to pray as individuals, but this left him at a loss. At home, Sally had always led their family prayers. Then at church, the group prayers were led by either the pastor or one of the deacons. Still, Stan tried to keep a reverent train of thought as he sought to pray for those around him. But his mind seemed unable to focus. In the back of his mind, he could sense the Spirit moving through the silent church. Like an unfelt breeze passing first one way, then another. The feeling was so strong that it brought to mind the time he and Sally went to the coast the year before. He had waded out into the surf where he could feel the gentle, yet strong wave action. First, pulling at him as though it wanted him to go further out to sea, then pushing back toward the shore, as if he were intruding upon the wave's environment.

Then an impertinent thought struck Stan, pulling him out of his enjoyment in feeling the Spirit's movements. Just as his feelings of the Spirit began to fade, he thought, *'I wonder what's keeping Brenda silent? I've never known her to keep silent when the Spirit is moving, much less this strongly?'* Then, as if on cue, Brenda leapt up from where she had knelt and gave two very quick cryptic outbursts before collapsing into a weeping mass on the floor. Stan shifted slightly so that he could see where Brenda lay to assure himself that she was all right. The outbursts had been so unlike the long, song-like flow of syllables and sounds that would leave Stan feeling good. This outburst left a nagging feeling in the back of Stan's mind, almost a foreboding, as he waited and listened for William, who had always interpreted for Brenda's speaking in tongues. While he waited, Stan's mind quickly ran over the controversy of Bill's allowing Brenda to practice what he called a gift of the Spirit. Bill had pointed out Paul's restrictions toward the speaking of tongues in the Bible, and that since there was an interpreter, there should be no complaint. Stan smiled to himself, as he remembered the flustered faces of the men who had opposed it from the beginning. *'After all,'* Stan thought, *'How can you argue with Scripture?'* And there had never been any arguing as to Bill's knowledge of the Scriptures or what they meant.

Stan's mind quickly returned to the present, as he heard something from William who was sitting two rows up from him. Looking up, Stan could see that William was crying. Concentrating, he could barely make out William saying, "I'm sorry...I can't....I'm sorry,...so sorry...."

"William? What is it? Is that what she said?" When William turned around to respond to Stan's questions, Stan could see tears making their way down his cheek. "No, Stan," he said in a near whisper. "And I'm afraid I am the fraud." He looked back to his sister, sitting silently beside him. "Wilma is the interpreter, not me."

Stan thought for a second. *Wilma?* The young lady was always soft spoken, but William had always said that it was more than that. Come to think of it, he thought that he remembered William telling him once that she had injured her throat and could never speak above a whisper.

"What she said was, 'Why did you wait?...Why did you wait?'...I'm afraid, Stan...so afraid. I think ... maybe it's too late." Even as he finished, William turned back to the kneeling form of his sister. Crying silently, he leaned on the back of the pew in front of him.

Stan very carefully sat up, not wishing to disturb those still praying around him, and looked around at the kneeling church. There was a strange silence throughout the church. Even the outside sounds failed to reach Stan where he sat. It was as if the whole world was holding its breath. Looking up front, he noticed that Brother Danny had deserted his perch and was no longer looking down at Brother Bill. In fact, Stan couldn't see any sign of the large music director anywhere. Still, something about the silence nagged at the back of Stan's mind like a thought not quite completed and yet recently forgotten. In a hushed tone, he whispered to his wife while still looking around, "What do you suppose it all means, Sally?" When he didn't receive a response, he looked down, thinking that his wife had not heard him, and repeated a little louder, "...Sally?" Something about her stillness bothered

Stan, but he couldn't think of what it might be. Gently, he lifted her face and looked into her eyes to get her attention. The expression of rapture upon her face was so total and complete, it sent a warm feeling through Stan. He found himself smiling childishly at his wife. Still, that nagging feeling that something wasn't right wouldn't go away. "What is it?" he asked in a hushed whisper, more to himself than to her. There was something to do with her lack of response that seemed to hold the key to the nagging feeling at the back of his mind. Then slowly, as if each fact was drifting independently through the jelly-like mist of his mind, they began to come together: the abnormal stillness, the frozen expression, (even if it was one of an ultimate joy) the slightly glazed stare of her eyes, the unusual feeling that this wasn't Sally. *'That's absurd, of course...this...is...Sally?'* he thought, as his mind shifted back to the fixed stare...of...her...eyes. Something seemed to click inside Stan's mind like a small door being opened. A door that he didn't want to look inside of but was being drawn toward, as if he had no control over what he was doing. Over and over again, his mind replayed the pictures his eyes saw, each time denying what was hiding behind that slowly opening door.

Finally, after what could have been hours or seconds,(Stan couldn't have known either way) his mind saw what the eyes had been seeing. Somewhere inside his mind, Stan grabbed hold of the door and looked within.

Like a little boy who throws open his closet door at night to prove to himself that there is no such thing as monsters. Only to find that the monster facing him is worse than he thought. He was frozen. A distant part somewhere far away told him that he still sat in Tucamill's only Baptist church-that it was Sunday-that all his friends were here-that he was alive. As the thought, *'I've been left behind...,'* slowly filtered into his conscious mind, that part of him that was struggling to hold on, *...snapped.* The sound that erupted from his throat to shatter the silence was one of such pure anguish and pain, that it brought up heads as though they were pulled by hidden strings. Not every head came up, however, for it seemed a good third of the church still remained in their kneeling position.

The events that immediately followed Stan's cry seemed to drift by him in a fog. Like they were happening to somebody else, somebody very distant. Someone was screaming, **"THE PLAGUE...PLAGUE,"** while others were simply screaming. He saw Sarah, a teenage single parent, who had been in the church about a month. She was shaking her 3 month-old baby. Distantly, Stan thought, *'she shouldn't do that, she might hurt the baby'* until she threw the small bundle away from her and ran out screaming. The church became a milling mass of chaos, as people scrambled over the still-kneeling forms of those who had not moved. Some, who apparently feared even touching the bodies that were being shoved aside, scrambled over the backs of the pews. Those who had bothered to make it to the aisles, clawed and crowded each other, as everyone tried to be the first to reach the back exit.

'*Funny,*' a detached thought came to Stan, '*I wonder why no one is trying to go out the doors behind the pulpit?*' With excessive care, Stan carefully shifted Sally's still form from its kneeling position next to him, up into his lap. Without even realizing what he was doing, he rose slowly to his feet and began moving down the pew toward the aisle. Through the fog of his mind, Stan could remember apologizing to those who still knelt in prayer, as he jostled his way down toward the aisle. He didn't realize he had anything in his arms, until McDoule appeared in front of him. He was shaking Stan by the shoulders, but what he was saying didn't make any sense.

Through the fog of his mind, Stan could hear McDoule shouting, "There's nothing you can do! We've got to get out of here! Drop it, and lets get out of here!" Looking down, Stan realized that he was carrying Sally as cautiously as he could, and that McDoule seemed to be trying to make him drop his wife. Shifting, so as to put his body between Sally and McDoule, Stan looked at the church deacon with confusion. Stan could only think that what McDoule was saying didn't make any sense to him at all. Before his fog-shrouded mind could put together the words, to ask what McDoule meant, another familiar face entered into Stan's field of vision.

It was William. He had a hand on M{c}Doule's arm and was saying, "Leave him, Rodney. Can't you see that he's had enough?" Stan couldn't see the force William had applied, to get Rodney to release him. But he did see William's face after Rodney M{c}Doule had left him. The look on William's face was a combination of compassion and sadness, as their eyes met. Then his face vanished into the shroud of fog that held the chaos around Stan at a distance. Faces drifted in and out of Stan's field of vision, as he made his way against the tide, not really knowing where he was going. Until finally, the sounds of confusion seemed to fade, and Stan found himself at the front of the sanctuary, looking down where his friend Bill knelt next to the pulpit. With as much care as Stan had ever done anything, he shifted Sally in his arms, as he turned and sat beside Bill on the raised platform next to the pulpit.

Slowly, Stan began to survey the now-quiet church that seemed to stretch out before him with an unnatural stillness. The main door at the back of the sanctuary stood slightly ajar, letting in a thin band of sunlight that ran nearly the length of the main aisle. Stan shook his head to try and dispel the nagging feeling of disorientation that was interfering with his thinking. He could see the scattered backs of those who still knelt in their pews, along with a few, still forms that lay along the main aisle, where they had unceremoniously been pushed during the mad exodus. An exodus that had turned the most peaceful church service that Stan could ever remember, into mindless chaos. Stan could only assume that there were bodies along the outer aisles as well. Then his eyes fell upon Brenda's still form, slumped at the end of one of the pews. It took a moment for Stan to realize that she lay too still for the living. With a smile, he whispered, "No need to weep now, Brenda. You've made it." Then he began surveying the three front pews of the church. Nearly each pew was fully occupied down its full length. There were a few vacant places where a person may have knelt to pray, before they realized that the person next to them no longer needed the prayers.

Looking along the first row of pews, Stan smiled, as his eyes fell upon the Anderson boys, with Amy's arms still stretched protectively over each shoulder. Nearby, knelt Fern, with her hands still clutched in the hands of her close friend, Gertrude. Stan could see where the tears had streaked the makeup of her face, as the two had prayed together.

A little farther down knelt Dorien, the teenage girls' Sunday school teacher. She knelt alone with a vacant spot next to her. Stan wondered if the person that she came to pray with couldn't let go of their past. Or more importantly, if she had come forward to get her heart back on track, and the person who had joined her, didn't. So his survey went passing from person to person, feeling happy for those he saw kneeling in place, and saddened by each vacant place. Until at last his mind brought him to where he sat, next to his friend Bill.

"Who would have guessed, Bill? Not me, that's for sure. I guess I always believed like so many others, that when the time came there would be trumpets and the splitting of the clouds.... Or was that what it was like for you? And to think He gave us a chance, right up to the last...and in your words, no less. No,...no one can say God didn't give us every opportunity." With that, Stan's eyes dropped to Sally's head which he cradled in his lap. He had thought that he had cried himself out. Felt sure that there were no more tears to cry. Yet the tears began anew, flowing freely down his cheeks to fall upon his wife's upturned face. A face that still held the joyous rapture that she surely felt when she left his world behind.

Realizing his tears were marring Sally's make-up, Stan stopped the absent-minded stroking of her hair long enough to dry her face with his kerchief. "I'm sorry, Sally...I didn't mean to mess up your make-up. Even with that, your face is still the most perfect face I've ever seen." Again, Stan's sorrow clutched at his throat and chest, pulling sobs through the numbness that had come after he had first cried himself out. "Oh, Sally, can you ever forgive me? We both felt so strongly that when our time came, we would go together. I never even considered the possibility that I might not be ready." As he cried out, his sobs became more prevalent to the point that had anyone been there, they wouldn't have been able to understand his words. "It wasn't you...my treasured Sally. It was my own arrogant pride that has separated us! Oh, sweet Jesus, forgive me!"

Gasping from his sobbed outburst, Stan stopped and thought. As he recovered from the outburst, he began talking in a melancholy tone that drifted off to that of a soft whisper. "No, I mustn't think about that....It's too late for me. Jesus, watch over my Sally....Please. Nothing else matters now, nothing but her happiness. Much better me than her, if we must be separated."

"Stan ... Stan ...Stan," the soft voice interrupted Stan's thoughts. Before looking up, Stan had to wipe the tears from his eyes before he could see. *'Is this some trick of the mind?'* he thought. The person before him, dressed all in white, seemed to waver slightly in his vision. Somewhere, the back of his mind registered the red-orange flames that were working their way up the back wall of the sanctuary. But like so many other thoughts, thoughts of flames quickly faded as he regarded the person before him. The building around Stan seemed to fade somehow, as this stranger stepped forward. Stan couldn't help but feel he knew this *[man?]* from somewhere. "Stan...." the person began again. Only this time his voice seemed stronger than before. "Stan, there's someone waiting for you....Come." With that, the stranger reached his hand out for Stan to take. Without thinking, Stan lifted his hand up to the man before him. As he did, he could feel his world of sorrow being consumed by an unimaginable joy.

* * * * * * * * * * * * * * * *

Drifting aimlessly through the crowd gathered to watch the old church burn, William took little notice of the gaunt looks of shock that so many of the faces held. Something of the numbness that held him began to fade, as he came upon a group in earnest conversation. The words that caught William's attention were from someone saying, "We have more than enough in the building fund to replace the old building. What we need is a leader, someone who can take charge, and lead like a good pastor should." Looking around, he found a group of four deacons. Rodney McDoule and Andrew Willards were alternating as though each was the chief deacon for the church, speaking with Danny Hankins, the music director.

Danny's response addressed the group with no less pride than if he addressed an entire congregation: "Well, Gentlemen, as you know, I am a fully ordained minister. And I am quite capable of standing up to the task at hand, even if some in the past have failed to appreciate my qualifications. Still, were I asked to step in during the church's darkest hour, I must have the assurance of the full support of the church elders. Not that I am presuming...or anything of the nature.... In fact, I don't think I could even be able to give this matter a serious thought, until I was officially approached." The murmurs that accompanied the nodding heads of the four deacons were still too low for William to hear as he moved closer. Not so, for the speech Danny was presenting. It seemed the longer he spoke, the louder he was becoming, as if to make sure that those around him heard as he continued: "Still, I must say that the leaders of the church must stand together. It is a unity that the people need now more than ever. Not just for the church, but the whole community as well. No indeed, this is no time for hesitation. The people need the support of a strong church, a church with a strong leadership in this time of despair."

William had reached the group now which was beginning to gather quite an audience. So William had no difficulty in hearing Rodney's much quieter tone as he said, "And no more of this New Age nonsense." A woman nearby who had also heard, gasped, "What are you saying?"

Rodney turned on the lady with enough suddenness to make her step back, and replied, "Why do you think God struck down Bill?" Then continuing in a more relaxed tone, he continued, "No, God doesn't punish those who are doing what he wants them to. No, Bill had brought the New Age into the church when he first tolerated that woman with her *speaking in tongues*."

At the mention of "New Age," several gasps went around the crowd. Stienburg, one of the more moderate, surviving deacons, spoke up. "Don't get us wrong," was Stienburg's contribution to the conversation. "We had a great deal of respect for our former pastor. As you can see yourself, we now realize that we shouldn't have been as lax as we were. Who knows what we might have forestalled, had we not given in to the more...shall we say, liberal members of our church?" The short speech was punctuated by the crashing of timbers. As the burning church building finally collapsed in on itself.

As though the collapsing building was a release to his shock, not only of what he had been through, but for what he was hearing as well, William could no longer hold his tongue. To the crowd at large, he called, "What's wrong with you people? Don't you realize what is going on here?" Then more directly, he focused on the small group that had been addressing the crowd: "And you...you're supposed to be our leaders. You're supposed to give us spiritual guidance, not drag people from the face of God. Can you really be so dense, that you really don't know what is going on here? Don't you have any idea at all?"

"Now see here, William," Andrews broke in, "You have no right to speak to us in that tone of voice." William had been as surprised at his own outburst as anyone else. But that surprise, came nowhere near his surprise, as to the quick and venomous reaction he was receiving. A compounding form of shock seemed to settle in even deeper, as the stern-voiced deacon that he had once considered a friend, continued his relentless attack. "We **are** the elders of the church, **not** you! And maybe you'd like to tell us how it is that you are here, when so many good men and women never left that building. Could it be that maybe *your master* isn't through using you in the corruption of us dedicated Christians?"

Before William had a chance to even consider recovery, Danny stepped up to join in the verbal attack on this possible source of opposition: "Listen, and listen well, William Holdstead. The time for you *and your kind* is past now. If you can't conform to the ways of the church, you'll be asked to leave. We are not trying to force anyone out of the congregation, but we cannot, and will not, tolerate dissension among the members." As he spoke, Danny's voice lowered in volume so that only William could hear him as he finished with, "The choice is yours, William. We realize that you're distraught right now but don't take too long in deciding. And don't go speaking out until you've had time to think about what I have said." Even on a good day, Danny's six foot six, two hundred seventy-something build could be intimidating. Now, with the red-faced anger of the large music director coming down on him, William found himself backing up without even realizing it.

Slowly, in a deeper shock than he had felt when he first realized what had happened in the church, William drifted out of the crowd. Looking back, he could see an ever-growing congregation of people around Danny and the four deacons. Tears began anew, as he turned away and whispered to himself, "I guess he's right. The time for me and my kind has indeed passed."   The smoke from the burning church seemed to somehow dim the very sunlight, that had been so bright and cheerful not three hours gone.

CHAPTER TWO

Heaven's Flame

The Hernandez family sat quietly around the low coffee table in the living room of their adopted home. In the light of a single candle, John Hernandez read from the Bible that they had found on this very table upon moving in. Heavy curtains on the windows kept anyone on the outside from glimpsing the candle's light. Still, John read quietly to prevent anyone passing in the night from hearing. He didn't think being awake would be considered a violation of the curfew, but he didn't want to be accused of doing anything to the home's owner. There was, after all, little tolerance for squatters in the community that they had adopted as their own.

A knock at the door froze everyone in place. John always took care to prevent anyone from seeing him return here from work, so no one could know he was here.

Still, a knock in the night was more than disturbing. The national curfew meant that anyone out at this time of night was either an enforcer of some kind or one of the many roaming gangs.

Closing the Bible quietly, he handed the book across the table to his wife. Taking in his wide-eyed children, John motioned everyone to keep silent and move back deeper into the house. Trying to keep the fear he felt from his face, John watched as his wife, Maria, gathered their two children and vanished into the shadows. That taken care of, he took up the candle and made his way slowly to the front door. Pausing at the door, John listened a moment to make sure that there was no sound to betray those he loved, to whomever had come to call.

Opening the door slowly, John felt his fear soar. The middle-aged man standing patiently in the doorway was not wearing the uniform of an enforcer, nor was he alone. Although the group didn't look like the typical gang, including the elderly, the children, and everything between, he couldn't think of it being anything else. Not that he had ever heard of a gang as large as this.

Suddenly, John realized that the man standing before him was looking at his hands. He could do nothing about the hand holding the candle, but he quickly slipped his other hand into his pocket. As the stranger looked into his eyes, John wondered if it was his face that the man studied or his forehead. Either way, John felt more self-conscious of his lack of a registration mark than ever before.

To cover for this lack, John blurted, "I didn't steal anything." Then realizing how that sounded, he added, "The house was empty when I got here."

Then another thought struck John. One more fearful than the possibility of a neighborhood watch group investigating the house. He might have been born and raised in America, but his Hispanic heritage was plain to any who looked. Then, there was the lack of an official registration mark. Was that what this tired-looking gentleman was searching for? Over the last couple of years, he had seen many of his kindred persecuted and even killed outright. And this had all the look of a lynching mob to John, despite the presence of children.

"Be at peace," the tired-looking gentleman said.

At the same time, he made a calming, pacifying gesture. "My name is Rick and God has sent me."

John hadn't thought he could be more frightened than he already was. But at those words, John realized that he had been wrong. He felt as if his life's blood was draining from his face, looking again at the size of the group gathered in the front yard. A lynching mob might be satisfied to take his life and leave. But a group of religious fanatics would want to purify the house as well. And there were enough here to surround the entire house if they thought someone might try to escape through a side door. He had heard enough tales of the like. And even that some of the local churches were looking for people to blame for recent catastrophes.

Trying to relax, John thought faster than he ever had in his life. If he could keep them engaged, then maybe they wouldn't consider looking for anyone else. He had taken great care to keep his family hidden. There was no way they could know that he wasn't alone. Everyone seemed to be out front. And if he did nothing to make them think otherwise, his family should be able to slip out the back door before the house was burnt. Silently, he prayed that Maria would be able to keep their children quiet when the crowd finally decided to lay hands on him.

Instead of denouncing him as an alien as John expected, Rick just shook his head. And in the light of the candle, John could see a deep sadness spread across Rick's face. Exposing a face that looked to have seen more than any one person could endure, yet continued to hold on through shear determination. "You are thinking we are of the church, aren't you?"

"No, not at all," John lied. He thought he was better at hiding his feelings than this. So how could this stranger see through him so easily?

"That's all right. I too, have seen some of the atrocities committed by churches in God's name. And if I thought that they were after me, I might feel the same kind of fear I see on your face. We are not of the church. We are of God. So be at peace."

"You are Christians?" At Rick's nod, John felt even more confused. "How can you be Christians and not be of the church? The church is the Christians."

To John's surprise, the sadness in Rick's face only deepened. Looking off toward a steeple visible above some of the neighborhood treetops, the moonlight seemed to make that spire glow in the night. Still, Rick only shook his head.

"It is true they call themselves Christians. But they are no more Christian than that rock," Rick said, pointing to a decorative stone to one side of the porch. "They use God's Word to justify their terrible acts without ever truly reading what the Word says. They claim the authority of Christ's blood, and at the same time, they deny God's very existence in their own hearts."

Looking deep into John's eyes as if he could see into his heart, Rick finished. "No matter their words or the titles they claim, the people of the church are not Christian. And the god they follow is not Christ. Their god is the god of this world."

"Then why come to me? Do you think I have something to do with the church?"

"Not at all. As I said, God sent me. He spoke to me this very night, saying that I was to gather in all His children. God said that His wrath would mark this night, and I was to lead His children to safety."

"I am not what you say. I am just a simple factory worker, trying to earn a living."

"You may want me to believe that or even believe it yourself, but the Lord has spoken. And He never misdirects His children. He told me of your coming, and how you found the Word. That in the finding, you have found the truth of the Word. The Word is in your heart now, and that makes you a child of God." Looking past John to the darkness of the house, he added, "And in your new life, you have brought your own family into God's family."

The emotions and sensations that rose up in John were almost too overpowering for him to grasp. Fear, joy, excitement, and even anxiety seemed to be tripping over themselves within his mind. This was like one of those stories he had read in the Bible. Where God spoke to His people, sending them out on mysterious missions. But John had lived in the real world long enough to have doubts. Then, some of what Rick had said penetrated beyond his desire to be part of this kind of family. How could this man, or anyone for that matter, know of his family?

"What do you mean?" John demanded, fearing for his family's sake. Then, realizing he couldn't bring them into this without confirming their existence, John turned to another part of Rick's statement. "How could I find any kind of Word?"

"I don't know. He spoke His Word to me, then led me here. I can only suspect you found something that has shown you the truth of God's Word. Maybe even a Freedom Bible."

John felt stricken at the mention of a Bible. Could the words of that book really be real? But even if they were, how could this man know anything about it?

Rick smiled as if he had read John's mind, then continued: "It would be like Simpson. Not many of us were willing to keep a real copy near the end, given the penalty. But then, Simpson would have counted any penalty a small cost for the sake of God's Word."

"I don't know any Simpson," John began defensively. Then a chilled thought came. *'Could that be the home's real owner? What if they think I did something to this Simpson?'* "I didn't do anything wrong. The house was empty when I found it."

"Peace...be still," Rick said, making a placating gesture. "I knew Simpson. He was a good man and a friend of mine. More importantly, I know you have done nothing wrong. This was his house before being taken up. And a greater man of faith, I have never known."

Rick paused as if thinking of something distasteful, looking about at the others before continuing with his explanation. "He tried to warn us, you know. But we wouldn't listen. He knew the day was coming. But try as he did, he could never make us listen. And the end result was that we were not ready when the day of the Lord came. It was our lack of faith that left us behind - which was not the case with Simpson."

One of the men spoke up from the shadows. "How could you know he would be right? Simpson and his family may have been good and Godly people but they were just part of the church. He wasn't educated up in the Word like an elder or priest. How could anyone expect him to know more than the collective clergy of the town?"

Something beyond understanding pulled every eye to the heavens. A strange, off-colored shooting star streaked across the sky - followed shortly after by a faint, yet eerie sound that seemed to raise the hairs on the back of John's neck. Before he could turn away, a second shooting star appeared. This one seemed brighter, leaving a faint, blue-green, after-image across the sky even as it vanished.

For some reason John couldn't understand, the sight of those two lights filled him with a sense of dread. He had seen many shooting stars in his life, but this seemed somehow different. Was it the angle of descent? They did seem to be coming in much steeper than any he could remember. Was it that chilling color following the second? He couldn't remember ever seeing one of such a color before. Maybe it was that sound that seemed to penetrate the skull beyond hearing. John wasn't an astronomer to consider such things, so why the fear now?

"We must leave. Now! Call your family out quickly." Something seemed to have affected Rick by the fear in his voice - a fear that seemed to have a contagion of its own. A fear that seemed to override John's reluctance.

"Why? What's going on?"

"Judgment." Rick took a quick glance at the sky, then at those behind him, before continuing. "I was instructed to gather in all those the Lord named and flee to the mountains."

"But my friends. What will happen to them?"

"There is no time. We leave now." With another weary glance to the sky, Rick added, "We can talk on the way."

"Maria!" John called back into the house. "We're leaving! Bring the children."

When John's wife came out of the darkness, she did so hesitantly. Their two children clutched Maria's skirt as they walked silently behind their mother. Maria's hands gripped the Bible to her chest like a shield. Despite her attempt to hide it, Maria's paleness betrayed her fear.

As she stopped short, their 10 year old son, Andrew, stepped forward. Sensing the tension, Andrew stood with both fists clinched, as if he could protect his mother from the assembled crowd beyond the doorway. Their daughter, on the other hand, buried her face in Maria's skirt behind her back.

John felt a strong desire to comfort his family, to tell them that this was not a lynch mob. But Rick's fear had infected him and John could only think of getting away from this place.

"We'll leave that behind," John said, pointing to the Bible held tightly in his wife's hands. "Maybe someone else will find their way through it." John caught a faint smile touching Rick's face as he spoke. But the smile was gone almost as quickly as it came.

"But where will we go?" Fear raised Maria's voice an octave, but the voice remained otherwise steady. John had always been proud of his wife's strength, but never so much as he felt at this moment.

"With them," indicating the group gathered in the front yard. "They are going to a place of safety."

"We came to help." Rick spoke up in an urgent tone. "But to do so, we must leave now. I was told the lights in the sky would mark the beginning." Another greenish streak, brighter than the earlier ones, seemed to punctuate his words with its barely audible whistle as it passed overhead. "Quickly now, time is growing short."

With Genia still clinging to her skirt, Maria rushed to the short, round table in the house's den. Placing the Bible in the table's center with a care that belayed her urgency, Maria then took her daughter's hand and rushed back to join John. John motioned Andrew to take his mother's other hand, then turned to join Rick, already stepping away from the doorway. With family in tow, John turned his back on the place they had called home for the last year.

****

It was a quiet group that followed Rick along the darkened streets. John never gave a second thought to the few possessions he had accumulated and left behind. His mind was focused on following Rick to this place of safety. For like the others, he had become infected by the same fear that seemed to hold them all in silence.

Since they were traveling through a residential district, the streets remained dark, although the glow of the industrial and commercial districts could be seen above the rooftops. As part of the energy regulatory system, only essential districts were allowed 24 hour access to electrical energy. Of course, with the local power grid being shut down for the night, the group had a good view of the increasing celestial events. The moon provided the group a pale light by which to make their way through the night. The moon's light was occasionally tinted with a soft, blue-green flare as the falling stars began to become brighter and more frequent.

An increase in the lights streaking across the sky only intensified the fear that gripped the group. And shoulders began to hunch when the brightness indicated that one of those objects had come very close. From time to time, various members of the group would look up to watch an object streak across the sky, without swerve or hesitation. Another change, along with the increase in brightness, was the sound. As the objects became brighter and closer, the auditory effect began to climb from a barely audible vibration to a deep, moan-like noise – a sound that seemed to chill each one of the group down to their soul.

Feeling a desire to break the fear-induced silence of the group, and take his own mind off of what was flying overhead, John moved close to Rick. He took care not to distract the man who seemed to be feeling his way along the twisting course they all followed through the night.

"What will become of my friends?" John asked, as they were making their way down a straight stretch of street. "Is there nothing I can do?" An exceptionally bright object streaking overhead without a sound, seemed to emphasize John's question.

"I'm sorry, no," Rick said, as he stopped at the next intersection. He looked both ways as if he didn't know the way, or was listening to some unspoken direction. Motioning everyone to the left street, he added, "God has given us this opportunity to stand aside. But there is nothing we can do to alter His judgment."

A hollow thud seemed to punctuate Rick's statement. John's head appeared to turn of its own accord to locate the sound. One of the objects had impacted the earth somewhere off to their right. *We would have been about there, had Rick not turned us when he did.* A flaring, blue-green fireball marked where the impact must have been. But despite the nearness of the impact, no sound from the ball of flame reached the group. John wasn't sure which was more frightening: the objects that moaned across the sky or those that made no sound at all.

"Do not go in among the homes," Rick said urgently. "Our safety lies along the course the Lord has set for us. Touch nothing and stay together."

It was not long before John decided that it wasn't the shooting stars that held the real fear, after all. Before the group had gone half-way down the block, the night erupted into chaos. The occasional crashing sounds of timbers from fire-consumed structures were suddenly drowned out, as people began pouring out of their homes screaming in terror. Screams that seemed to stop John's heart with their chill. Yet despite the terrified cries, John's first thought was, '*how could so many people dare to defy the federal curfew*'? Then the absurdity of the thought struck him, leaving John numbed.

Walking through the fear-filled night, John felt a strange, unnatural calm possess him. Stumbling along before regaining his sense of balance, John followed Rick through a night lit by the ever increasing number of falling objects. He felt sure that the real estate-consuming flames would bring him no harm. Still, a sadness filled his heart over the fear-stricken faces that fled past the group. People that rushed by as if they were unaware of the group's presence.

Then, one of those screaming men was someone John recognized. They had worked together for almost a year and John considered the man a friend. John started to reach out as the man rushed by, but he felt a restraining hand from behind. And the man was gone, rushing across the street, even as he continued screaming. Nor was he alone in his mad rush, joining a large crowd as it converged on the neighborhood church.

John froze along with most of the group, watching in horror as a blue-green fireball consumed the entire building. A grand structure just moments before, when the door closed behind the last person, was now little more than a large pile of rubble. The charred and smoking timbers looking like some mysterious animal's skeletal remains. In the shock of what had just occurred, the world seemed silent. If there were still cries in the night, John's traumatized mind could no longer register them.

Stumbling up alongside Rick, John stammered, "How could God destroy His own church? And with people in it too."

"I know." Rick's voice held a sadness that was in stark contrast to the grim determination on his face. "But then, that was not God's church. That church had believed the lie. Those within have long followed without thought or discernment. Now there is nothing we can do. They chose to believe in an abstract god who would accept whatever they wished. Now they must face the judgment of the very God they had for years denied."

"But the church? There must be someplace that is safe."

"The church is not a building. It never was. That

belief helped lead so many into the lie. And now it's too late." Motioning for John and the others to keep up, Rick picked up the pace. As they made their way down the street, he continued, "The church is God's people, not the building. God's people were the dwelling place of the Holy Spirit. The building has never been more than a worldly structure to meet in. As for safety? There is no safety. Nor will there be, until Christ walks the earth once again. But if we continue to follow Him and keep our faith in the Lord, then He will see us through to the end."

From the looks that passed among those around him, it was apparent to John that this was something new to the group. Yet even with this pessimistic declaration, no one seemed inclined to leave. And John realized that like them, he too, felt an acceptance of this prospect. With an almost fatalistic conviction, they continued to follow Rick into the night.

As they continued on though, John was beginning to wonder if even Rick knew where they were going. The course he led them along seemed to be haphazard. It tracked back and forth through darkened neighborhoods and well-lit commercial districts without any apparent rationale. Still, they did seem to be slowly working their way eastward. Rick would stop at each intersection, as if listening to some unheard voice, before leading them down the next street.

The night still shook with the deep vibrations of continuous impacts. But despite all irrationality, the group seemed to always find the safest path through the town. There was ample evidence of recent impacts. And they heard impacts in almost every direction. Yet none of the objects seemed to fall close enough to be a threat.

Turning the corner onto a well-lit street, John recognized the strip-mall across the street. This was the last commercial district along the east edge of town. John had been here many times over the last year, but he had never been beyond it. Out there was the abandoned countryside. The street lights kept the area bright, even though the district was closed to the public after dark.

"No!" Came a scream from someone near the back of the group. Everyone froze at that heartfelt cry. Then, the woman who had cried out, yelled once again, "Marcus, NO!"

It seemed every other head turned to see what was happening. But instead of looking back toward the source, John's attention was arrested at seeing a large gang of teenagers. The gang was coming up an alley almost directly across from the group. Colored bands of cloth, marking the gang's affiliation, became visible as they entered the well-lit parking lot. Looking about cautiously, the gang reminded John of a pack of skittish coyotes, hunting the last chicken. Miraculously, the gang failed to see the group of believers – or even to hear the woman's scream. Even as the gang kept a close lookout for authorities, they began working on the glass store-front. In short order, they had a large portion of the window broken out, while managing to keep the security strip intact.

Finally looking back, John saw a dark-haired woman moving up toward Rick. "I have to," She pleaded. "He's my son." John didn't think he had ever seen anyone with such an expression of desperation before.

Rick never answered. Instead, he closed his eyes, turning his head heavenward as if to pray. John was sure that he saw a tear glisten in the streetlight's glare on Rick's cheek.

Breaking away from the group, the woman began to run toward the store. She quickly made it across the street, but the gang had already vanished through the broken window. As she ran, the lady continued to cry for her Marcus to come back. Despite her racket, it was obvious to John that the gang members still did not hear the lady. He could still see the unconcerned movements of teenagers among the store's merchandise.

Suddenly, a brilliant flash robbed John of sight. The greenish light was so intense that it numbed John's mind to the point that he was barely aware of the wave of warm air rushing over him. When vision returned, John was momentarily confused. Then he realized that what had been a shopping center moments before, was now a shadowed heap of rubble. The street lights were no longer providing their discriminatory illumination. It took a moment with the diminished lighting to locate the dark-haired lady, or at least what remained. Even in the dim lighting, John could make out smoke rising from the supine form. Her feet extended toward the rubble pile with one arm reaching outward. That arm must have been reaching toward the store when the object struck. But now, it was to the heavens that it reached.

"We must leave...now." The gruffness in Rick's voice could have come from pain or even anger. But a quick look at Rick's face with its tear-stained cheeks, told John that this was from an anguish even beyond pain. Noone made a sound as Rick led them quickly down the street with most averting their eyes so that they would not see the lady's remains. With eyes on the ground, it was easier not to see what they were passing through.

****

For what seemed an hour or more, the group marched through the night in silence. There were no sounds of wildlife in this strange, otherworldly night. The waning moon provided enough illumination for them to see the road they followed, occasionally augmented by the greenish glow of the meteoric objects passing overhead.

The road was relatively straight with cleared fields on either side. The random valleys were filled with darkened woods that became deeper and larger, the further they got from the town. The land also began changing with the distance from the town. The fields became smaller with steeper climbs for the valley walls until they were traveling through what must have been a forest.

Finally, Rick motioned for everyone to stop. Pointing off to one side of the road, a barely discernable drive followed the narrow ridge they were now on. With a second glance, John noticed a line of faint lights marking the path. This part of the area had long since been removed from the power-grid, so where could the light be coming from? Then, as the group turned off the road to follow the dimly lit path, John took a closer look and realized that these were solar lights that had somehow managed to maintain their function. The lights along the main path were fading rapidly, while those that passed near to the trees were now dark.

After nearly a quarter of a mile, the group came out in a clearing that overlooked one of the steeper valleys. In the clearing's middle stood a darkened structure. The only thing that John could make out in the darkness was the shape of a large building of some kind. It wasn't until they got closer that he could identify it as a house. It must have belonged to some wealthy land-baron to be so large and tucked away as it was in the woods.

With a self-assurance that seemed to radiate from him, Rick led the group up to the front door. Motioning for the others to stay back, he tried the door. His relief was notable as the door knob turned with a small click.

The door was unlocked. Pushing it inward, Rick stepped into the darkness of the home's entry with John close behind. Looking to the left, Rick shook his head as if arguing with himself, then shrugged before reaching out to flip a light switch. A number of people gasped as the entry light came on. After the darkness of the night, the sudden light seemed brilliant. However, after a few seconds of adaptation, John was able to see the glow of the wire filament within the bulb. Something he had never seen before.

"What could make a light do that?" John asked, pointing to the bulb.

"There is very little current," someone said, behind him. "My guess would be that the house has been off the grid for some time. Possibly using solar power cells with battery backup. The batteries must be running low. Either that, or something is acting as a power drain."

"Here we go," Rick said, locating a collection of flashlights on a side-shelf. Stepping over, he began passing out the lights as the group began filtering into the entry way.

Taking the first light, John stepped deeper into the dark home, turning on his light as he made room for the next in line. At first, the light seemed bright, until John realized that the brightness was only relative to the entry light. The flashlight's battery must be worn out. As the variety of flashlights were turned on, someone flipped off the overhead light to conserve the home's power. Looking back, John was amazed to see that the last light went to the last person to enter. It was as if the house had been prepared for them. John then began a cursory exploration.

"It seems the owners had been Christian," John called back, as he started to enter a dining room off to the left. "There is a Bible on the table."

John wasn't sure just what he had expected, but it most certainly wasn't the reactions that came from behind. He heard a number of gasps as he started into the room. Looking back, he saw Genia grab Maria's skirt as she picked up the fear from the other adults. He might expect this kind of response from an announcement of a serpent, but surely not the Word of God.

"John, don't move!" Rick called. "Dennis, you and Albert check it out."

The identified men rushed forward with their flashlights. One flashlight seemed to out- shine John's and the other one combined. John's amazement at the light's brightness was replaced by shock. He noticed Rick and a few others praying in hushed tones, looking back to the two men as they rushed by.

By their quiet conversations, John identified the man with the bright light as Albert. Albert located a pencil on the floor. Then handed his light over to Dennis. With Dennis illuminating the table top, Albert very carefully used the pencil to flip the cover of the book open as if he expected to find a real serpent on those pages. Then using the eraser, he carefully flipped the pages back until the cover page was exposed. After a thorough examination, Albert smiled and closed the Bible by hand.

"It's all right," he called. "The publication date is 1988. It's real."

"I don't understand," John said, stepping up to Albert's side. "Aren't all Bibles real?"

"You don't know, do you?" Albert looked deep into John's face, using his bright light as if it could help him see into John's mind. After a short breath, he continued, "No, not every Bible is real. In fact, possession of a Freedom Bible is a federal offense."

"Freedom Bible? Someone said something about a Freedom Bible earlier."

"That is what we call Bibles printed before the TIL law was enacted. That's the 'Tolerance in Literature' law, by the way. The law prohibited the printing of any Christian material felt to be offensive. Regulators mandated a revision of all Bibles printed after the law's enactment, removing those verses contradicting the politically inclusive attitude of the time. The law also prohibited the possession of any Christian Bible in print prior to the law's enactment."

Dennis took up the explanation. "Had this been a PC Bible, we would have been sure that the home had not been left by a Christian, and might very well have been a trap." At John's blank look, Dennis added, "We call those Bibles printed after the enactment of the TIL law, 'PC'

Bibles. Had that been one of those, we would not want to touch it. We've heard of other places thought to be refuges only to be traps set up by the state, usually activated by someone picking up the suspected Bible."

"But that is not the case here, thank God." Rick spoke as he joined the group at the table. "The government began implementation of the TIL law about a year before the Lord called his people home." Rick must have noticed John's confusion, for he went on to explain, "The media called it a plague."

"The plague?"

"The media couldn't admit to the people that the Lord had come for His bride, now could they? For one, there wasn't anybody left in the media that even believed that God existed. Secondly, they had spent decades trying to purge God from our society. After all that, they were hardly going to admit that the God that they had been denying might have a role in the mysterious loss of millions of people across the globe."

"Where does that leave us?" John felt a chill as if his very spirit had just been cast adrift. "If He has taken His people out of the world, are we abandoned then?"

"Of course not. What the Word says about God's children hasn't changed. He still loves us. But He had provided specific criteria that we were to comply with if we were to escape these times." Rick spoke while looking at the others, making their way deeper into the house with their lights scanning for hidden dangers. "Christ still loves us. But we weren't ready when He came for us. Because of that, we must endure the darkness of these times. And then, there are people like you. That you could find a Freedom Bible and through that book, find the Lord. That gives me hope beyond anything I have seen since the Spirit departed from this world. It's just one more proof of His Word. And that gives me hope that His return is soon."

"But I thought that was when the Lord would call His people to be with Him in the clouds?"

"That event is what we used to call 'the rapture.' Though I doubt the word would be enough for those called up. It's definitely not a word those of us left behind want to think about too much. With the rapture came a departure of the Holy Spirit's involvement in this world. I'm talking about Christ's return to claim His earthly throne"

"I'm not familiar with that," John said, looking at the book sitting tantalizingly at the table's edge. "Where is it at?"

"We'll look it up together," Albert offered. "In the light of day. We have a copy of the Word and now it seems we have a place of refuge. What more could we ask for? Right, Rick?"

"True enough. Though I cannot be sure that this is our place of safety. We might have to leave come morning. After we've had a chance to see where we are."

"If it was the Lord who brought us here, wouldn't he have had a reason?" John looked at the two men next to him expectantly. He felt certain that this night had just proved the reality of the God in the Bible. Why would this leader, who seemed to know so much, speak as if there might be doubt?

"You are right." Rick looked John in the eyes while nodding to himself. "It was the Lord who led us here. And He never does anything without a reason. Come first light, we will give thanks for the deliverance of this night. And then, we will follow Albert's suggestion. We will open the Word and find all the messages that we have missed.

****

As night turns to day, and days turn to weeks, life goes on even during times of trial and judgment. During the days following the harrowing night of terror, John found himself falling into a routine with his newly adopted family. It didn't take John long to realize that this place of refuge seemed perfectly set up for their group once they had settled.

Albert proved well versed in many of the books in the home's library. Dennis seemed to know everything there was to know about home repair and was able to address the many small issues that plagued a home long-abandoned. Then, there was Bartly, who as an electrical engineer, knew about the solar panels used to power the home and how to reconstitute the batteries that stored electricity for nighttime use as well. There was a mechanic who was able to repair the variety of damages inflicted upon the many devices found. As nature had afflicted many of them over the last few years. There was even an electrician who reconnected the solar panels, repairing lines that had broken when neglect allowed them to shift. And there was Rick, of course, who not only held the group together, but seemed to know everything there was to know about the Bible.

The only one that didn't seem to have a specific purpose in their new home was John. Even John's own son, Andrew, had demonstrated his worth. His early curious explorations uncovered a secreted cache of hunting supplies. Equipment that had long since been outlawed by federal mandate. Equipment that now provided the group with the ability to obtain foodstuffs without the need to leave the relative safety of their refuge.

After a week of frustration, John finally voiced his concern to Rick. "I can't help feeling that I'm useless. It seems that everyone else has a place. For every problem, there seems to be someone with the necessary skills to address it. But I don't have any skills. Why would the Lord need me here? I just hold everyone back."

"Nonsense. Everyone here had a life before the Lord's day. A life that helped us make it in the world. Our failure was not to prepare in the Spirit. That is why we were all left behind. In His love, the Lord brought us to this house. A refuge He prepared for us. But that alone couldn't change our hearts. The Holy Spirit would have taken care of that, but He is gone now. What you bring to this family is more important than all the safety and luxuries placed before us. You bring a hunger for the Word. You have shown us what we have missed for so long - how to really love the Word."

"How can my ignorance help anyone?"

"There is an old saying. To truly learn something, teach it to another. I can only believe that the Lord knew of my failings. Because like the others here, He prepared us with the specific skills we would need. But that was not enough, although it wasn't until you joined us that I began to realize it. In you, we can all see what we lost in our pursuit of bettering ourselves. Each of us had that same hunger, that same desire in our early days. You are helping us find it again."

"But you were a preacher. How could you not know?"

"It was the religion that got in the way. I served the created, not the Creator. Look at all the preachers around today. You don't think they came to their position after the Lord's day, do you? No, they were like me. They knew the words and the way of the Lord, but they didn't know the Lord. The only thing that sets me apart from them is that I realized what had happened - even if it was too late."

"But you're here now, right? You're teaching us now. Could that be why you were left?"

"Bless you, no. At one time I had tried to romanticize my situation, to convince myself of that. But the Lord sent His angel to set me straight. My sin is mine. And my teachings had only managed to provide hope and hold the group together. Then the Lord brought you in, and your desire and love has put a fire in us for the Word."

****

Three weeks after their arrival, Albert was able to share one of his talents with the group. As they gathered for their evening Bible reading and study, John realized that someone was missing. Rick had already opened the Bible but was looking about to identify the missing member. That was when Albert slipped into the room by the back door. This was unlike Albert. The man was never late, not even on days when it was his turn for hunting detail. So if Albert was in the back of the house, what had kept him?

There was something in Albert's eyes. A faint look of excitement was there, yet there seemed to be a sadness as well. Rick calmly closed the Bible and turned to Albert as did everyone else in the room.

"I got the computer working," Albert announced. "And the satellite dish was old enough that I was able to tap into the internet without a registration number. Apparently, they didn't shut down the older network interfaces when the regulatory system took effect."

"There is something else though, isn't there?" Rick asked, "What is it?" With his ability to see into the heart of any conversation, it was easy to see why Rick was the group's leader. Even had the man not been a preacher, he would have undoubtedly been the one to take charge. Then again, he may have noticed the frown lines that John was just noticing on Albert's face.

"While I was on, I decided to search the news. It has been so long since we have heard of anything overseas." Albert looked about the room with a puzzled expression. "It seems they have rebuilt the Temple in Jerusalem. One report stated that the Chief Magistrate of the UN was to dedicate the Temple for service in three days. The article says that the traditional day of Jewish mourning will now be a time for celebration. With the Ninth of Av marking the opening of the newly built Temple of Israel. The report indicates some discontent among the Jewish population of Israel. It says most are thrilled with the UN's intervention allowing the Temple's rebuilding. Then, it states that there is a small number of malcontents who are demanding that the Temple be consecrated by the Rabbinical leadership instead of the UN's Chief Magistrate."

"They've rebuilt the Temple?" John wasn't sure, but it sounded like Weston's voice coming from the back of the room.

"It must be so," Rick said, while holding his hand up for silence. "We'll have to look it up. I know there is something in the Word about the Temple being rebuilt, but I can't remember at the moment. But there is more. Isn't there?"

"Yes," Albert said in a cautionary voice. "It seems the UN declared that it was necessary for the UN's Magistrate of Religion to perform the dedication for the sake of peace. They claimed that the new Temple was to represent all religions and not just the Jews."

Rick nodded, but he only continued to stare at Albert. John was sure that there was something going on here, but he couldn't imagine what it might be. Rick had never interrupted their Bible lessons, except for the occasional sharing sessions. And even if this was a source of news believed to have been lost to them, it didn't seem enough to cancel their nightly routine. There must be more to it than what had been said so far.

"Found a number of reports about the continued incursions of pestilence. They are saying that the invading insects that are moving up from the southern states have come up with the peoples fleeing through the Central American corridor. Not that anyone can prove or disprove the claim. Any chance of monitoring that kind of migration ended with the dismantling of the Mexican-American border."

"How could that affect us?" Sorien asked, with a concerned look on his face. "Even if the pestilence is moving with the people, we are well out of the way here."

"I know, but it seems the President of the South-American Union is calling the reports a ruse. She claims these reports are an attempt to justify a pending invasion, and is calling for her people to rise up and defend their national sovereignty."

"That could get messy," Bartly offered, from his seat against the wall.

"The Brazilian governor has gone on record to support this claim, by saying that there has never been an insect to match the claims of the CDC. That either the North-American Union has fabricated the whole tale, or some bio-weapon has been released to help work the peoples up. I also found a report that describes the insects. I don't believe I have ever seen such a bizarre bug. And the report speaks of bites causing boils that defy all medical intervention."

"I don't believe I have ever heard such dire news," said Rick. "But that can't be what has your face so stiff." Rick motioned Albert forward to hand him a tissue, to dab tears that John hadn't realized that Albert was shedding. "What has happened?"

"They found a group of Believers up near Quebec." Albert had to stop to clear his throat before continuing, "They had a Freedom Bible."

Every eye turned to the Bible resting in its place of honor in the middle of the table. It was as if the book itself had become a magnet, pulling their attention. Yet while all other eyes were on the book, Rick asked the needed question. And John realized that this was the news that Albert feared to speak. Though John couldn't imagine why.

"And how did they respond?"

"They are home now." As if that cryptic response was answer enough, everyone's head bowed.

Taking the words literally, John smiled. After all, what could be better than going home? Not that John had ever known what home meant, before joining this group.

"Why the sadness? They are together, right?" John couldn't keep the joy out of his voice, thinking only of his own joy at being with a true family. Even if something didn't seem to fit, what could be wrong with this news?

"You're right. He's right," Rick said, to the rest of the room, addressing the strange looks being directed at John. "We should be celebrating. Though I think John should know why."

"It's something about the Freedom Bible, isn't it? I remember you saying something about the Freedom Bible the night we met. But what does that have to do with this?"

"The prohibition against the Freedom Bible declares its very possession a capital crime, a hate crime. And to have one marks you as a terrorist to the state."

"But why? There is nothing in here that promotes hate or violence," John said, pointing to the Bible. "I have read enough to know that hate and violence both are prohibited by the Word."

"That has never been the point. It is an issue of truth and control. The Bible speaks in absolutes and truth, telling us that there is only one way to repentance. This challenges the validity of the state Bible. It also contradicts the UN's mandate declaring all religions the same."

"I never heard anything about this. How could something like this happen?"

"It did not happen overnight. The specific laws concerning the Freedom Bible were established in a series of apparently unrelated amendments added to larger laws, enacted over a period of years."

"But didn't anyone notice what was happening?"

"How could they? The amendments were never enacted. They were just random sections to a meaningless law. They were just idle words on a page. Until the last of the laws were enacted, and then it was too late. The various amendments were pulled out of the various bills and laws and consolidated almost overnight. Once the full law was reformulated into its final form, it was fearfully enforced. For unlike other laws, this one came with very specific criteria to identify the offense and the mandated penalties. The next morning, the people of America woke up to find the Bible itself proscribed. With the publishing houses required to adopt acceptable editing for any Bible to be printed."

John was stricken. How could the government that he had respected be so sinister? He had always liked the United States - even before it was expanded to include the former Canadian and Mexican lands under its legal umbrella. And he had seen the expansion as an opportunity for his father's people. Now he wasn't so sure.

"You see, anyone caught with a Freedom Bible is given a choice," Rick added, even as John looked to Albert.

"You said the group was home?" John asked. Though now, he wasn't sure he really wanted to hear the answer.

"The government doesn't want to appear unforgiving to the masses," someone added from the back of the room. John was too stunned by this point to even try to identify the speaker.

Albert looked back, nodding to the speaker, before responding, "First, you are called upon to renounce anything found within your Bible. Then, you are called upon to accept reeducation. The purpose of which is to assure that your conversion is legal. For among other points, you must fully renounce any belief in Christ. If you fail to comply to even one of the points, the law mandates an immediate execution - specifically decapitation."

"The Word challenges the legitimacy of the government," Dennis added. "Just like the old American constitution, the Bible points to God as the only legitimate authority to issue the rights of man."

"What Albert had meant," Rick said, looking at the others to forestall any more interruptions, "Is that particular group had chosen not to renounce Christ. In doing so, they now stand among the ranks of brothers and sisters who have gone before us."

For the first time since the terrible night that brought John and his family to this wonderful place of refuge, John felt truly afraid. Looking to his wife standing among the other women, he could see his own fears mirrored on Maria's face. His mind was numb as he turned back to Rick.

"Now, you know the full extent of the danger you face here. The choice is yours, just know that you are making it for your family as well. No matter what you decide, we will always love you," Rick said, nodding to both John and Maria. "If you stay, you face the same risk as those found in Quebec. If you leave, no one will try to stop you."

Looking at all the faces around him, even back to the wall, John knew that Rick spoke truth. All he saw was love and understanding on those faces. And he knew that any one of these people would lay their life down to protect John and his family. This was what it really meant to be a part of a family.

"Where would I go? What would I do?"

"You have survived up until now without the mark. You could always take the mark. Join the ranks of registered workers. The future is for you to choose."

"I can't. I mean, I couldn't leave my family behind. And you are all my family now." Suddenly, John had to wipe his own eyes, using his sleeve. "Besides, from what you have read, to take the mark is a renouncement of God in itself. Why would I dare forsake Him? It was He who saved us all on that terrible night of fire and death. No other God has ever offered anything for me or my children. The God of Heaven not only offered His protection, He showed me that He was capable of supplying that protection."

With his declaration, John realized that the tension in the room had not been his alone. Although he was sure that the tension of his new family was for him and not for themselves. For suddenly everyone was on their feet, rushing toward both John and Maria.

The room seemed to be a chaos of love. John found himself being soundly patted and hugged and even his hands grasped all at the same time. Looking over some of the shorter heads, John could see his wife receiving the same show of affection. And he had to blink away the tears that were clouding his vision. Not even among his own family as a young boy, had John ever felt so accepted, so loved. Looking over, he saw Rick standing back to let the group gather around their newest members. Tears ran down Rick's cheeks as well, although he held his composure. But the look of rapture made their leader's face glow, as he looked back and forth between John and Maria.

"John, Maria," Rick began, as the room became hushed once again. "We may not be home yet. But short of the day when we can walk with the Lord, I doubt I will ever know any more joy than I know at this moment. Most of us were raised with the Word, even if we didn't fully believe. We were left behind because of our own failings. The two of you, on the other hand, never knew God's love or hope. Where we floundered back to the Way, the two of you have truly found the Way. I feel as if my heart could fly to know that you and your family are part of God's family."

Taking John's hand, Rick reached the other toward Maria to join them. "Let us sing. This is a time for rejoicing. Let Christ hear the joy He has given us here." With that, the whole group began to sing a deep, resonating song. John vaguely recognized it as one of the Psalms he had read before he had ever known that others might believe in this same God. Then, he realized that among the various voices that had often been sung during their Bible time, he was hearing Rick's deep, rich voice.

A sound John had never heard before. For this was the first time he had ever heard the man sing out.

72

CHAPTER THREE

The King's Return

The scent of freshly tilled soil floated on the gentle breeze, drifting across the mid-western landscape. Enjoying the afternoon, Benjamin sat on his case of seed, overlooking his own plot of land. The surrounding fields were already planted with the community cash crop and waiting on the coming spring rains. But the forty acres allotted to Benjamin were still awaiting the planting.

Benjamin had asked the equipment operators to till all of his land this year before they moved on to other fields. He then spent the last two weeks planting the fields around him along with the neighboring farmers. Now, he had time to lay out his crop. It would be another week before the rains were scheduled to move across this part of the land, so he had time to get everything in place. Not like the old days when rains came on their own timing, and were just as likely to drown a crop as water it, usually resulting in a harvest shortfall. No, it was nothing like the old days, thanks to the King and His coming. These days, there was always plenty of food. And that was even with the rotational cycle for the fields.

Benjamin needed the extra crop this year. Where the two-thirds rule was plenty for their needs, it left little for luxuries - and this year, Benjamin intended to plant with a specific luxury in mind. The case containing the seed for their personal foods was already set aside at the site for their food garden. Now, he needed to plan the layout before moving the cases to the appointed sections of the field. The extra planted twelve acres should provide enough to do something really special for his wife, Laura, while giving his land the next year off. It had been a long time since he had gotten something truly special, and he had just the gift in mind. If he could just keep it a secret from Laura until after harvest time.

The smell of the rich, black mid-western soil was something unique from all the lands he had traveled. But that rich smell often reminded Benjamin of the time before the land was reclaimed When the soil always had a dry, gritty odor while seeming to resist the crops struggling people tried to wring from it. Benjamin wasn't sure, but he thought the land had changed the year before the King's return. The great western eruption had buried the entire mid-western America under dozens of feet of ash and tectonic materials. A tribulation disaster that turned to a blessing of new life and hope with the King's return.

"Grandpa! Grandpa!" Came a child's voice across the field. Looking around, Benjamin saw his favorite grandson running up the mile-long drive from the main road. Even as he caught sight of the young man, Jason was climbing over the fence and began angling across the field to where Benjamin sat.

"Off the dirt, Lad," Benjamin called to him, motioning to the strip of grass that separated the section of his allotted grounds. The seeds might not be in the ground yet, but he didn't want the soil trampled until they were. And then, he would want to protect the fragile seed crop. Jason was a good boy, he just needed to be reminded from time to time. The winter had beaten the sod down, making it into a good path for the youngster anyway. Nodding in satisfaction at his grandson's compliance, he looked back up the road even as he asked, "So, where are your parents, Young Man?"

Benjamin was sure he would have heard the auto, even if his son had let the boy out at the main road. "Back at home packing," said Jason, responding with all the excitement a 13 year-old could muster. Winded as he was, Jason's voice was as jubilant as ever.

"You came alone?" Benjamin asked, as he motioned for his grandson to have a seat on an unopened crate of seed next to the crate he was sitting on. "Five miles is a long way for someone your age to travel alone."

He couldn't keep the concern out of his voice, although he did his best.

"Oh, Grandpa...you know it's safe. After all, what would hurt me?"

Feeling somewhat chastised, Benjamin admitted, "What, indeed. You're right. We live in peaceful times these days. But it's still a long walk for someone your age. So, what brings you here today?"

"We're going to Jerusalem!" No one can do excitement better than a 13 year-old boy and at this point, Jason was outdoing himself. "They had a contest at school, you see, and I won! The first prize was an all-expense paid trip to Jerusalem! Mom and Dad said it was all right, as long as I didn't fall behind in my school. So we're going as soon as the school year ends! Isn't that great?"

"I'm proud of you, Son. But tell me, what was the contest? It had to be something, to have such a grand prize."

"It was an essay contest. We had to write a paper on what it would be like to visit the Capital. Some of the kids thought that they meant the American Capital City, but I got it right! The real Capital City in Jerusalem! I knew Mom and Dad have never been there, and I thought, 'wouldn't it be great if we could all go together?' Dad said you went there once, but that was a very long time ago. He said you don't talk about it much." Jason cocked his head in confusion over such a thought. He couldn't imagine anyone not sharing an experience. "Anyway, I wrote what it would be like to meet the King."

"Now that is a goal anyone of any age could appreciate. And I couldn't imagine a greater experience for you or your parents." Benjamin smiled as he ruffled his grandson's hair. "But remember, meeting the King is not something to be taken lightly. He is not like anyone you have ever met. There are also many protocols attached to any such meetings. You don't want to make any mistakes if you do get the chance to meet the King Himself."

"I know," Jason said, with enough seriousness to make any adult proud. "I studied all the texts on how to present myself. I even got a tutor from the city clergy to go over the things that the texts left out. And that turned out to be a lot." Looking a little sideways, he added, "the priest told me you would know more than most."

"Probably not. That was a long time ago, and the times were a bit different then."

"What do you mean?"

"Look at these fields." Benjamin waved his arm, indicating all of the tilled fields around them. "There was a time when the soil was dead and gray. It produced, but nothing like the fields of today. When the King came, He changed the world, giving it a new life. My experiences were from when that new life was at its beginning."

"What does that have to do with anything?"

"It was the curse. A little over a hundred years ago, the people of this land began turning their hearts against God. The land was turned over to an all-dominating government. History no longer records the fickle hearts of the American people of that time. But if you look closely, you can see how their attitudes and actions brought on the curse that stripped these lands of their native richness."

"Do you mean the dust bowl? I read about it last year. But that was a long time ago. How could that have anything to do with what you know about seeing the King?"

"You're right about it being a long time ago. But it is the best demonstration of the world's curse and its restoration. You are a part of the restored world. What I experienced could hardly apply to what you might face going before the King."

"How could losing all that soil be about restoration?"

"Simple enough. During the dark times there was a great eruption out West. The results...," Benjamin waved an arm toward the fields one more time. "Restored much of the soil cast off during the dust bowl. The result was a new lease on life for the land, although it didn't start to truly prosper until the King Himself returned."

"Wow, you really do know everything."

With a smile, Benjamin shook his head. But before he could respond, a call from the house announced that dinner was ready.

Rising, Benjamin gave his grandson a warm hug before motioning him on ahead. Before he started to the house, Jason made Benjamin promise to let him tell his grandmother the good news. Shaking his head, Benjamin smiled as Jason ran on ahead. Gathering the tools that were sitting out at the garden's gate, he detoured to the tool shed next to the house before continuing on in.

"Grandma! Grandma, guess what?" Jason cried, as he ran on into the house, just as Benjamin was reaching the front porch.

As Benjamin entered the front door, he heard his grandson engaging Laura in a detailed explanation of the contest. Much more than he had told Benjamin of earlier. He was even throwing inside notes about his essay, and how he had come up with the various ideas he presented. Smiling at the infectiousness of the young man's behavior, Benjamin sat quietly at the end of the dinner table.

Laura managed to give her full attention to their grandson's tale, so as not to interrupt him. All the while she moved about, setting the evening table around him. Her heartfelt murmurs of acclamation and encouragement only acted to feed Jason's excitement. So much that he never noticed her placing the settings at the chair he stood next to. Included were two of his favorites alongside the empty plates: peach pie, which she had to have gathered the makings from the winter cellar, and sweet bread, both of which were time-consuming to make. Obviously, Benjamin's son, or more likely, daughter-in-law, had called ahead to give notice.

Benjamin's smile increased as he thought about this little behind-the-scenes conspiracy. He, of course, had to be kept in the dark, he was sure. How else could he play his role when Jason broke the news?

Eventually, Jason began to wind down and his level of excitement dropped enough that the smell of the meal laid out before them penetrated his awareness. Looking at the table, Jason's eyes grew wide and his cheeks turned the color of fire with his embarrassment. "I didn't mean...I mean I don't want to interrupt your dinner. I'm sorry, I didn't realize it was time to eat." Then his eyes seemed to lock of their own accord on the loaf of sweet bread sitting next to the empty plate.

"Of course, Jason," Laura assured him. "You're much too nice to make us wait for our dinner. And besides, the meal is just now ready."

That was when Jason's eyes found the peach pie. "Ah...,Grandma, do you think there might be enough that I could ...maybe...have a bite?" His eyes never left the pie as he asked.

"Of course, Dear." Waving to the seat at his side, she added, "have a seat. Your mother and I have already spoken."

Jason paused just long enough to say, "Really, thank you, Grandma. I don't know what to say." As he spoke, Jason's eyes never left the pie. Nor was he gentle, as he dropped to his chair and began spooning dessert onto his plate. Like all young men of his age, when permitted, dessert preceded the meal.

"Don't get ahead of yourself, Jason," Benjamin admonished. "Let's say Grace first. And since it seems that you have the greatest honor to be thankful for, do you think you could say the Grace for the meal?"

Jason stammered slightly, then raised his chin and rose to the moment. Although the prayer of thanksgiving was a bit disjointed, Benjamin couldn't have asked for a more heartfelt prayer from his grandson. With a smile, he loaded his own plate with meat and potatoes, as his wife filled a second plate with meat and vegetables for Jason. Laura slid it within his reach before filling her own plate.

While they all settled into eating their evening meal, conversation came to an end. Nor did Jason's gusto diminish with the consumption of his dessert. While Jason began on his main plate, Benjamin began picking up the empty dishes and started around the table toward the kitchen. Leaning down on the way by, he said to Laura, "I take it Jane called ahead."

Even though it was unlikely Jason would pay attention to anything until his meal was finished, Laura kept her voice low. "Yes, but I didn't have time to let you know. And then, I decided it would be better to let him surprise you."

Gathering up the rest of the dishes in front of Laura, he continued on to the kitchen sink. After washing the dishes, he met Laura at the door where she was bringing in the last of the dishes. He would normally have assisted in the remaining cleanup, but Benjamin's attention was demanded by Jason who was looking up expectantly from his seat.

At Benjamin's suggestion, the two moved into the living room where he started a small fire in the fireplace while waiting for Laura. Once there, she settled in her own reclining chair while Jason settled on the floor between it and Benjamin's handmade rocker. The small fire had taken the chill out of the air. The evening air was cool but not enough to require the furnace for comfort.

As they all relaxed, Jason looked up at his grandfather with a serious look on his face. As if he wasn't sure how to say what he wanted. This was very unlike Jason, who always spoke first and thought later. Then, finally, he opened his mouth before speaking in an overly soft voice. "Grandpa, what was it like?"

Benjamin looked down at his grandson who was lounging on the comforter beside his rocker. "What was what like?"

"When the King came. Dad said you were there, but that you don't talk about it much."

The question hit Benjamin hard. Ice seemed to be creeping up and down his spine. *'I should have known this was coming,'* he thought to himself. Especially with his grandson winning the contest allowing for his pilgrimage this summer. Still, he felt blind-sided somehow. Looking over, he saw the concern in Laura's eyes and realized that his feelings weren't as well hidden as he thought. He couldn't imagine what his face looked like, but it was enough to concern the love of his life. Jason looked worried as well. His expression said he knew that he had said something wrong but wasn't sure what. "Your father is right..." Benjamin tried to smile but wasn't sure if he was pulling it off. "But not about everything. I saw the sky open up and the host descend upon the land. But the King didn't come down in America. I did have my chance a bit later to make my pilgrimage to the Holy City, but all the action was over by then."

That didn't seem to settle Jason's concerned expression, so Benjamin tried again. "I haven't talked about those times much, because of the pain. I still have the memories, but I try to focus on the world as it is now. Still, I guess it's a human thing, the avoiding talking about the dark times. They say the veterans of the previous world war, World War II, were much the same. It is said that those brave souls seldom, if ever, spoke of the hell they witnessed during that war. They saw the evils that true Humanism could inflict upon man. Who knows, if they had spoken of what they had seen and experienced, maybe the American people wouldn't have been so quick to accept the same humanistic rule for America? But then again, they didn't have a divine governance overseeing their world to prevent the false narrative from being spread."

Jason seemed to relax a little, although he still had an expression of uncertainty. But now it was more as if he didn't understand what his grandfather was talking about, instead of concern over what he had done wrong. So Benjamin decided to try one more time. "I was speaking of war. Though fortunately, that is one thing you will never have to experience. And you may be right. It may be the time to talk about what happened back then. We can never know what would have happened had those veterans of that earlier world war spoke out. But that is no reason for me to follow their example."

"What are you talking about?"

"Excuses, I guess. But mostly what the world was like when the King returned. If He hadn't come when He did, I don't know what would have happened, or if the world itself would have survived, for they were indeed dark times."

"You mean you were there too? I thought everyone who went through the dark times was forced to take the mark or die."

"Things weren't quite that clear then. If you rejected the mark, you were killed, that is true. But not everyone was asked to take the mark. If you weren't given the choice, then you couldn't refuse - a little loophole within the world law at the time."

"Is that why you don't talk about it?" Benjamin could see the excitement in his grandson's eyes and he knew what the lad was thinking.

"No, no. If you're thinking that I was some kind of resistance fighter, I definitely was not. By that time, those who would have become resistance fighters were long gone. Those who were left behind...." At the blank look on Jason's face, Benjamin added, "those who weren't called up with the great calling. Those left to the new world order either went into hiding or were swept up in one of the many deceptions of the time."

"Why weren't you called, Grandpa?"

"I could give you all the excuses that I told myself over those years. The truth is, I wasn't ready. I had heard the stories. Even read some of the Bible, but they were just stories to me. I didn't realize the truth of those stories until I was in the middle of them, and then it was too late."

"I thought everyone who knew Christ was called."

"Like I said, things were not so clear near the end of the Age of the Gentiles. The churches taught many things. Not all of which followed the Scriptures. What they called the 'lay people' followed the church leaders blindly, never looking to the Word to see if the teachings were true. I'm afraid I was one of those. It seemed that the more gifted of my contemporaries who followed the Christian faith were stronger in the Word than most preachers. Even those who stood alone without a church to call home. I guess that is why they were ready, while I and so many church goers found ourselves living through our worst nightmares."

"So how was it that you weren't put to the question?" Jason seemed intrigued and even more determined than before to hear the story.

"I had a skill that the leaders wanted." Benjamin smiled at the quizzical expression on his grandson's face. "The American space program had long since been disbanded when the great calling occurred. But the government at the time never allowed information that they might need go to waste. They had kept a list of all those who had worked with the program and what they were capable of. It didn't take long for the new leaders to declare the American constitution an antiquated and outdated document."

"What do you mean? They abandoned the American constitution?"

"As I said, those who would have stood up to such a move had already been called up. The new government in America was relegated a place in the world order, but its leaders saw only opportunity. They knew what they wanted, and to accomplish that task they needed people with very specific skills. I was one of those rounded up.'To serve the people's needs' as they put it at the time."

"You don't sound like it was a very good thing. Why wouldn't you have wanted to serve the people?"

"It was never about the people. The land was ruled by the humanistic government of the Beast at that time. I praise God that He chose to reinstate the American constitution after the King returned. And that you will never have to know the vileness of those self-serving people." At the look of confusion in Jason's eyes, Benjamin added, "In the eyes of a humanistic government, they considered the ruling class 'the people'. Those we would consider the people were considered subordinates or subjects. The humanists believed in the collective, which of course, was established to serve them."

The look on Jason's face became one of shock and disbelief, although he was not distracted from the tale itself. "But what did they want you for?"

"Weapons. The new American government saw itself as the world's salvation. It felt that of all the world's governments within the new order, it was the most progressive. It was the one that should be looked to, to hold this new world together, to lead them all. But to gain dominance over the other regions, America required weapons that would allow it to impose its enlightenment on the rest of the globe."

"Those of us with the requisite skills and knowledge were gathered together. The universities had already been closed and abandoned. This made for the perfect internment camps for those of us who had been collected."

"What are requisite skills?"

"The education level, along with the specific training that they thought could produce what they wanted. Of those rounded up with me, I knew three or four who were nuclear physicists, four aeronautical engineers, a couple of design engineers, and I was one of three astrophysicists."

"But why would they close the universities? And why use them for internment camps?"

"Once the world order was put in place, it was felt that there was no longer a need for the universities and colleges. The people were trained in accordance to the government's needs. And the last thing the government wanted was an educated populace. And as to why they used them for the internment camps? That is easy enough. When the universities were abandoned, they left all their equipment in place. The larger ones along the east coast had walled campuses. Many of which had been fortified before their closure to keep the street violence out."

"That sounds terrible."

"It was. But that is what this world had become without God. The great calling merely removed those who wanted to stand in the way of this darkness. As for the universities, those same walls that were made to keep violence out did very well to keep us in. We were the smartest people left alive in America at that time. We had everything: all the equipment we could ever want, unlimited resources and the government's blessing. All we had to do was create weapons to make the world tremble. Thinking back, I can't help but think that the government's own delusions were a kind of salvation for the world."

"That doesn't make any sense."

"The political leadership believed more in Hollywood than in science. Rather than concern themselves with what was possible, the governing body told us what we were to create. Of course, when we weren't able to produce those mythical weapons seen in Hollywood movies, the punishment was terrible. A number of my colleagues did lose their heads because of their failures. After a while, even the deluded leadership began to realize that they couldn't scare us into creating the impossible."

"But why did they need weapons? Was it for the last battle?"

"No. This was before everyone had united against Israel. The American government felt that if it had the greatest weaponry, it could once again rise to a position above all the others. That, and I think that they were afraid they wouldn't be able to defeat Israel when the time came."

"That can't be right. My history book says that America was Israel's strongest ally."

"Now Jason," Laura interjected. "I don't think...."

"That's all right," Benjamin told her, before turning his attention back to his grandson. "We have gone this far. Besides, he probably should know the truth about America during those times." Jason looked back and forth between his grandparents, unsure what they were talking about. But he seemed to realize that this was a sensitive subject.

"Like so many things from those times, nothing was absolute. But the Word read true where it said that every nation would rise up against the land of Israel. And yet you are right. Israel was America's greatest ally. Not that the new American government reciprocated in those feelings. It may have been out of appreciation for what America had done on behalf of Israel in its past. During the early years of the Jewish state, Israel relied heavily on the United States. And the two nations were the strongest allies that could be found anywhere. With time, America turned its back on Israel. And that left Israel as the one sovereign state against the entire new world order. But despite the betrayal, Israel never turned its back on the American people."

"What's the 'United States'? Did America have a different name back then?"

"That was one of the first changes to befall the United States after the abandonment of the constitution.

National sovereignty was put aside to form 'a greater union' as they called it. Before that time, America was three distinct nations. The King let it stay as one after His return, though they all had to accept the original American constitution. It was quite surprising to see what the constitution really was. The one I had lived under, after 150 years of manipulation, had lost the intent and meaning in so many ways. I guess that is what made it so easy to dispense of."

"Why would any nation allow itself to be erased?"

"Personally, I think it was an act of defiance against God and His Word. The Word stated that all nations were established by God. In dissolving nations and bringing them to their knees, the humanists could feel that they were greater than God. But that's getting off your original question about the relationship between Israel and America. For the most part, I and my fellow inventors were safe behind the walls of our elaborate prison. But we still had access to the internet at that time, and we kept tabs of what was going on in the outside world.

"The world at war had finally made its footprint felt across America, but the people were not alone. At the time, it seemed that only Israel bothered to monitor the threats that swept the globe. And they shared that information with the American government. Unfortunately, our government never shared the information with its people, and thousands died as a result. Rather than abandon the American people to whom Israel felt a kinship with, Israel began providing their intelligence directly to the people of America. Mostly, it was the local law enforcement agencies that relied on the information of pending terrorist attacks. But the citizens began following this flow of information as well. The results were a drastic decline in fatalities. Where there might have been thousands, attacks would only affect a few hundred. And many of those attacks were even prevented from happening by well-prepared officers with the support of an involved public."

"Why would any government let its people be attacked? That doesn't make sense."

"Too true. But then again, we lived in a very different world during the dark times. And it got worse. The leaders declared that anyone who accessed those intelligence sites must be traitors and spies. They used the fact that few of those who utilized the information provided by Israel died in the attacks as proof of their duplicity. Those local law agencies and officers not summarily executed were disbanded and replaced by loyal military units. Though to answer your question, who can say now what went on in the minds of those who had abandoned the laws of God? Does that help you?"

"Wow, even the books don't talk about that kind of stuff. They talk about people being forced to take the mark or die, but none of the rest of it. Were you in prison the whole time?"

"In the beginning, those who didn't have the requisite skills were given a chance to take the mark. But by the time they closed down the prisons, the leaders realized they needed a labor force to feed the masses. So by not giving their prisoners a chance at the mark, they had a slave labor force already in place. That is where I spent most of the dark times, harvesting crops as a conscripted worker."

"Is that where you were when the King returned? Was it really like what the books say?"

"It was the most wondrous event, and at the same time it was the most terrifying time of my life."

"Now, that really doesn't make any sense. How could it be wonderful and terrifying? Besides, after the dark times, how could their end be frightening?"

"I'm afraid even the King's return had its own fears. True, the dark times brought trials each and every day. But with the King's coming, everything was exposed. So much that I had taken for granted, for so long. Of everything I thought I knew, nothing turned out being as I believed. And the things I saw that day, they still give me a chill when they cross my mind."

"What was it like, Grandpa?" Jason seemed to perk up. It was as if he realized that they had reached the point he sought.

"I was in the fields with the other conscripted harvesters. I can't remember what we were harvesting at the time. It might have been squash or lettuce." As the long-forgotten memory began to surface, Benjamin felt a chill.

What's a conscripted harvester? Did you work one of the large field harvesters like they use today?"

"No. The government had outlawed the use of the harvest machines by that time. I don't remember the excuse given."

"You mean you had to harvest the fields by hand? Why would anyone want to do that? And how could you ever hope to bring in a harvest in time?"

"It was the law, then. I can't remember now whether it was over global warming or job creation. But the result was simple enough. And as for who would want to do it that way? We didn't have a choice. Anyone without the mark was relegated to working the fields." As he spoke, Benjamin felt himself slipping away. It was as if the world was changing around him. He sat looking down into his grandson's eyes, and yet his eyes seemed to see the fields around him once again. The smell of dirty people seemed to invade his mind, and the dry, gentle breeze of that long-ago moment seemed to brush his cheek.

A tiredness seemed to come over him as he continued speaking, not the tiredness of age, but the remembered fatigue of long hours under a baking sun. And in his mind, Benjamin once again stood among the other harvesters, bending to fill their individual sacks with withered cabbages.

****

The sky seemed especially clear, with the sun baking the workers even after the short water break. The few high clouds failed to diminish the sweltering heat of the day, or offer occasional shade as they passed beneath the sun. The air was so dry that it seemed to pull the moisture out of Benjamin through the very pores of his skin. It would be another hour before he was allowed another drink of water. And the only moisture left for him now was his sweat-soaked shirt. Along with well-placed sacks, the task-master stood over his section of the harvesters from the bed of the produce truck.

With quick chops of the hook knife, Benjamin cut the heads of cabbage free with one hand, while scooping the head into the waiting sack with the other. Moving steadily down the long rows, he kept his concentration on each stroke. He knew where the others were, but more importantly, a mishap with the knife wouldn't bring medical care. If that kind of mishap occurred, he would be lucky if he got supper that night.

In the last year or so, Benjamin had seen a number of his fellow harvesters left along the roadside at the end of the day. Left to fend for themselves if they didn't die outright, because they couldn't continue their work. A disabling injury would almost assure a shallow ditch for a grave if it came to that. Compassion was one of those long-abandoned myths of his childhood. No one today believed him when he spoke of how things used to be.

Benjamin's hand froze with the knife ready for its next chop. Something....maybe a shout from across the field pulled his head up. He wasn't really sure. Had someone missed with their knife? The task-masters wouldn't allow talking, much less shouting. It interfered with productivity.

Looking around, he saw his task-master standing up in the truck bed. But instead of watching the harvesters, he was looking off to the East. Looking to the East himself, Benjamin noted a number of people doing the same thing, although no one appeared to know what they were looking for. In his confusion, Benjamin stood up to see if his eyes could see what everyone else seemed to be missing: the source of the distraction. And no one was being called to task for the sudden lack of labor. It was as if there was something in the air that demanded their attention.

Then, there was something to look at. With every eye transfixed on the eastern sky, Benjamin saw a bright glow appear on the horizon. As bright as the mid-morning sun was, it didn't seem to diminish this new light. A chill ran through Benjamin, as the light rose above the horizon and began streaking across the sky like a great tongue of flame. Benjamin had never seen a flame so bright.

The flame seemed to move with an incredible speed as it continued in their direction. *"Could it be some kind of new missile?"* he thought, trying to rationalize what he was seeing. It couldn't be a plane caught fire, planes couldn't travel with the speed or altitude he was witnessing.

No. None of that made sense. The flames behind any kind of projectile would have a terminal end. This flame seemed to expand from its initial point into an ever expanding rift. As it neared, he could see runners streaking outward across the sky, increasing its expansion exponentially The first thought that came to his mind was that this was like someone torching a field and letting the flames run wild. Only the sky didn't burn, not like this.

In minutes, the tongue of flame had streaked from horizon to overhead, with Benjamin and the others standing transfixed in fear. *'What could do this? Is it the end?'* thought Benjamin, as the flame passed overhead, moving from east to west. Watching it streak across the sky made him think of how a knife might cut through the outer skin of a fruit. But in place of more flames within the widening streak above, a new sky was displayed. A sky that was clearer and more blue than any sky he could imagine. It was as if someone had cut through the sky itself, letting him see what the sky was meant to be.

As the leading edge of the flame passed, the runners and tears in the sky extended outward in each direction. It was as if someone had fractured the brittle surface of the sky and exposed cracks extending outward. It was easy to imagine that this new sky would soon encircle the entire globe. But as he watched this spread, he realized that there was more to that leading edge that he had failed to see initially. The edges of this spreading tear were not the glare of flame, but rather a thickness of light brighter than the flames that had already rolled beyond the horizon to the West. A light whose brightness defied any description his mind could conceive.

Looking on that light, Benjamin felt a shame overwhelm him, falling to his knees among the crop. The knife, long forgotten, fell uselessly to his side while he held a hand up to shield himself from that fearful light. Others around him seemed to have another reaction to the light. It was as if a madness had possessed the fields. All those around Benjamin began screaming out in anger and defiance. At the bizarre reaction from the other harvesters, Benjamin lowered his hand to see if they saw something he had missed.

Suddenly, Benjamin realized there was something else happening in the sky. With everything else happening, it shouldn't have been a surprise, and yet it was. The light lining the leading edge behind the flame seemed to become more substantial. As if instead of a single light, it was made up of countless individual points. With equal suddenness, those points of light began disengaging and streaking across the old sky toward the ground. Each streak moved with blinding speed, some along a straight line and others following a markedly erratic course. But each seemed to have its own destination. One of the streaks came right at Benjamin. Feeling certain that his death was at hand, Benjamin dropped his head to the ground and instinctively covered it with his hands. But strangely enough, he didn't feel fear. What he did feel was a growing, overpowering shame, the shame of all his failings, all the things he had left unfulfilled with his life.

Benjamin waited for the impact and his impending death from this bolt of light. But when nothing happened, he opened his eyes to see silvery boots standing next to him. Looking up, he saw a man in strange armor reaching down to offer him a hand up. Rather than take it, Benjamin scrambled to his feet on his own. Although it wasn't until he stood next to this strangely-attired man that he realized, *"I know this man. It's Stan...Stan Robinson."* He hadn't thought of his childhood friend since their lives had parted in college. The man only nodded before turning his attention toward the task-master standing in the truck bed. And the task-master's attention was definitely on the man standing next to Benjamin.

****

Benjamin was jerked back to the present by his grandson's excited voice. "What did he look like,

Grandpa? Was he really dressed in light like everyone says they are?"

It took a moment to realize what was happening. Nor was he really sure how much he had really said while his mind was locked in the lost memory. "I'm afraid 'everyone' is wrong. The guardians wear armor, not light. Though I guess, from a distance, the glow the armor gives off might be thought of as light." Benjamin tried to stay in the present with his grandson but the memory was too strong. It seemed to pull him back in against his will. He wasn't sure, but he felt certain the story he was telling was much less complete than the emotional onslaught he was experiencing.

****

"Your time has ended!" Stan declared, to the task-master. Although he seemed to be looking about as well, as if the declaration was for everyone there. "No longer will you be allowed to torment the King's children. For the King has returned to His rightful throne."

With that, the world around them seemed to explode in rage. The task-master pulled his revolver, one that Benjamin had never known him to miss with, and fired. Not at Stan, as Benjamin expected, but rather at Benjamin himself. Stan was already aware of the intended target. Shifting slightly, Stan held a gripped fist forward toward the task-master. It wasn't until he saw the reverberations in the air before him, that Benjamin realized his friend held a shield in that hand. A shield that seemed to stop the bullets without an impact effect. The bullets dropped harmlessly at Stan's feet. With the bullets gone, the task-master leaped from the truck bed and charged them, pulling a heavy bladed knife that he always kept at his side.

There was a scream nearby, and Benjamin turned to see Bambi looking directly at him. Gone were the smoky eyes and the not-so-veiled invitations for her comforts. Although he had always felt a wrongness in her overtures that had kept him from accepting her. It had been as if she had targeted him since the day that she had joined their harvester group. Now, her face was twisted and sharpened beyond that of natural anger or even rage. There was a beast-like insanity behind those eyes. Her lips pulled back to expose teeth that seemed to look more fang-like than he remembered. Even her hands were twisted, making her nails look more like claws in place of fingers. At that moment, Benjamin knew real fear.

As Bambi launched herself across the two intervening rows of produce toward Benjamin, Stan shifted. As he moved, Stan pulled what appeared to be some kind of sword, although like the shield, it didn't seem to have real substance. Substance or not, its impact was every bit as real as any steel sword in Benjamin's mind. The sword made a circular arc as it passed before Benjamin and through Bambi. The woman fell forward at his feet as Stan moved on to the next threat to Benjamin. It must have been an illusion, but he felt sure he had seen a faint shadow rip free as if it had been struck, and not Bambi.

Dropping back to his knees with tear-filled eyes, he looked upon the crumpled form of Bambi. His hands hovered over her still form, unsure of what he should do, much less what he wanted to do. Looking up, he saw Stan dancing about him, every stone, knife and the occasional bullet turned by that strangely transparent shield. And whenever anyone got too close, they were struck down. The bodies were building into a small mound around him. But they never got close to being able to reach either Stan or Benjamin. From this new angle, Benjamin noticed something about those who were struck down. With each, it was a single strike of the sword leaving a corpse to fall to the ground. There were no wounded about, just those attacking and those dead. Then, Benjamin noticed something else. As the sword struck, there seemed to be a slightly deformed shadow jerking free. As if it, and not the person, took the blow.

Staying down, Benjamin began looking around the field. And he noticed that he was not the only one to have picked up a protector. He could see four, maybe five, people in armor from his position. Each standing next to, or over their individual charge. One of the armored guards seemed to be shooting something. It was as if the person held a bow, but instead of arrows, streaks of light shot across the field taking down one attacker after another. It was all too much for his mind to process at the moment. And then he thought of something else, '*of the hundreds here, why are there so few being protected?*'

Turning back to Bambi's body, he slowly turned her over. To his surprise, there was no gaping wound across her body. And her face didn't have the expected contortion of pain. In fact, Benjamin didn't recognize her face at first. The sharp angular features were gone. The face was smoother, more rounded, softer, more attractive than it had been in life. And rather than pain or suffering, the face looked like that of a very tired person. It was as if she was more alive now than she had been while she walked among them.

A hand rested on his shoulder, pulling Benjamin's attention away from the lifeless form. "I'm sorry," Stan said, "but she has been gone a very long time. The young lady that she had been had made her peace with the world long ago. From that point, she ceased to be. Her body still walked the earth, but her spirit had died that day."

This time, Benjamin had to accept the helping hand to rise to his feet. He seemed overly weak. "Was there nothing you could do?" The tears almost choked him, thinking of this young woman who in death seemed more alive than when she lived.

"The Lord only gives us a choice. He does not mandate our response. For everyone who went into the darkness, it was up to them to make it out. Like everyone that fell here today, she had been warned. She chose the world." Benjamin could hear the sadness in his old friend's voice and knew it for sincerity.

"And me? No one came to me to give warning. Could I have faced the same fate?"

"Every warning was as individual as the person who received it. Yours kept you safe until the end. Then it was for me to see you safely into the new world."

Looking up for the first time since the chaos erupted, Benjamin noticed just how clear the sky really was. He had lived in a haze for so long. It was as if he had forgotten what a truly blue sky was like. There were no clouds, and yet the sun didn't burn. The very world itself was at peace. Even the air smelled fresher.

"Come now, Ben." Stan motioned for him to follow. "It's time for you to rest. The others will be seen to by their individual guardians. I'll take you to a safe place so you can rest and clean up. And I'm sure you will have many questions for me, but not here, I think. Then, when you're ready, we can go to the Holy City so you can meet the King."

****

The memory faded, allowing their small living room to come back into focus. Benjamin could feel tears leaking down his cheeks, and he could hear himself whimper, "Bambi...." Laura was looking at him with a pained expression. She was worried for him, he knew. That was the way she was. He didn't know how much he had really said, but he knew it wasn't everything. Jason was looking up with a confused look. Possibly for the pain Benjamin knew to be on his face, and possibly for the disjointed story he had no doubt presented.

"Did they really attack a guardian? Why would anyone want to do that? Didn't they know the guardians are here to help?"

"To them, the guardians were the enemy." Benjamin chose to hide the fact that he, and not the guardian, had been the real target. "They followed a master as surely as we follow the King today. And their master called on them to go to war."

"Surely the people knew these weren't everyday warriors they were facing. Or had they taken the mark?"

"The mark only saved the person for the final battle. Those who chose to make peace with the world without the mark.... They ceased to be who they were at that point. If they were who they had been before their fall, they might have turned aside when they saw the power of the guardian's weapons. But their master drove them on, even to the point of death itself. And that is how the world's power was broken."

"What do you mean 'the world's power'?" Jason looked over to the library, as if there might be some book that would explain this.

"The curse, of course. Stan explained it to me after that battle. The curse that had begun in the garden had finally come to an end. And now the world could finally be what it was meant to be."

"Stan...? You mean the guardian? Wow! You mean you really know a guardian? I never knew that. I bet Dad didn't even know that one. I can't believe it."

Benjamin smiled at Jason's excitement. The boy was truly distracted now by this latest revelation about his grandfather. The painful memories and their story would soon be forgotten, and they could get on with their lives once again. Jason now knew that the world before the King's return was far different from how the books presented it. And for once, Benjamin felt at peace with his memories. Maybe they would no longer haunt those nights when he was alone in the field. As he relaxed, he felt a new memory surfacing, one long forgotten from that same day. A memory that didn't carry the darkness and pain of that one event.

****

Well clear of the field, Stan sheathed his sword and took Benjamin by the arm. Then, with a smile, a light seemed to engulf the two of them. There seemed to be a faint sensation of movement before the light faded. Looking around, Benjamin found himself standing in the front yard of a long-abandoned house. Everything seemed overgrown or in disrepair. Then he recognized the house. It was his childhood home, not a half mile from where Stan himself had grown up.

"My old house has long been destroyed, but I thought you might remember this one."

With a smile, Benjamin invited Stan to join him, as he started toward the front door. And with a lightened heart, he realized that he was going to get the chance to entertain one of his oldest friends. Looking at Stan once again, while his childhood friend removed his helmet, he realized that Stan was somehow much younger than he himself felt. But then again, it was finally over, and he could rest at last.